Home Court
Is Where You Find It

WILLIAM R. COX

Dodd, Mead & Company ——————— New York

1   2   3   4   5   6   7   8   9   10

Library of Congress Cataloging in Publication Data

Cox, William Robert, date
   Home court is where you find it.

   SUMMARY: A 16-year-old basketball star from a
broken home who has been expelled from 3 schools in
California enters an eastern boarding school that has a
losing basketball team.
   [1. Basketball—Fiction.   2. Friendship—Fiction.
3. Boarding schools—Fiction.   4. School stories]
I. Title.
PZ7.C83942Ho   [Fic]   79-6641
ISBN 0-396-07798-6

To the best, loveliest editor
a writer could enjoy

Home Court
Is Where You Find It

I

WILLY CROWELL bounced the basketball, moved, dribbled right, left, between his legs, whirled and pumped it backwards, over his head, into the hoop. He retrieved it with one hand, spun it on his forefinger. His hair, blond from the sun, hung neatly over his ears and at the nape of his neck. He wore nothing but bathing shorts on his six-foot-three frame. His skin glistened. It was tanned, beach-tanned. His surfboard stood forlornly against the standard which upheld the basket. His father stood four-square and spoke in even tones.

"You are going east. Remember, you are sixteen, you are not a free soul, not even a free citizen. You have been expelled from three schools in California. Your habits are nonsocial, your attitude execrable. Your mother is disgusted with you."

Willy spoke for the first time. "Stepmother, please. I have no mother."

"You have a mother. She lives in New York. The relationship between you is beyond my control."

Willy went to the foul line. Without effort, almost without looking, he popped the ball through the basket.

His father said, "Your only expertise seems to be the ability to propel that leather sphere through yonder net. You don't have to work at it. Perhaps it will do something for you at Harper School, since they have a rotten team record over the last several years. It is almost time for you to get ready to make the plane. Have you anything to say before you leave?"

Willy paused to stare at his father. They were the same height, the same physical type, yet they were vastly different to the casual eye. "What's to say? You said it all."

He tried one more long shot. The ball arched, took wings, dropped through without disturbing the net. He took a last look at the surfboard. Then he walked past his father and entered the house and went up to his room. He stood for a moment staring out at the Pacific Ocean. Tiny figures rode the waves. There was a good surf, the sun shone. It was September but the sun was still bright and hot.

He turned away. He threw clothing into a backpack— jeans, pullover shirts, sandals, loafers, socks, shorts. A trunk had been sent ahead, and he could buy the garments necessary for a winter in New Jersey. There was a trust fund set up by his grandmother which allowed him that much independence. He sat down on his bed and assembled his thoughts.

It all came down to one fact: He had everything—but he had nothing.

2

WILLY CROWELL took a taxicab from Kennedy Airport, stuffing his backpack alongside him. The driver was loquacious.

"This here is the quickest route. You wanna go to Fifth Avenue east, right? Fancy joints there. You sure you got it right, kid?"

"I'm sure."

"You see them ruins? People used t' live in them places. Gone. Gov'ment money down the drain. You know who pays for them ruins? We do, kid, we do. It's a rip-off. Near as I can see, the whole schmear's a rip-off, you know?"

Willy said, "Is it?" And he thought maybe it was. His silence discouraged the driver. New York had not changed much at Fifth Avenue overlooking the park. He paid the man, tipping him two dollars. The driver seemed satisfied. Willy worried a lot about tipping, about not giving enough or giving too much.

The uniformed doorman at the apartment-condominium-whatever stared at him. It had been nearly four years, but it was still the same doorman. He looked at the sandals, the jeans, the pullover shirt. Then he beamed.

"Hey, your mother told me you were comin'. How you doin', Willy?"

"Okay."

"You don't just grow. You shoot up. Like a weed."

"Uh-huh." He was sensitive about his height excepting when he was on the basketball court. Contrariwise, when he had gone downtown in Los Angeles to try his skills against the real players he had felt like a midget.

"Let me call your ma." The doorman went inside. The lobby was marbled, high-ceilinged but not ornate. In a moment the elevator door opened and Willy went into the cage and the door slid closed and he touched the penthouse button. He felt odd in elevators; so much of California was built at ground level. When he got out he was in a private vestibule. A door opened and his mother came toward him, stopped in her tracks, stared up, her round blue eyes filled with amazement.

"Willy?"

"Yes, mother." He bent to kiss her, careful as always of her makeup. She was very beautiful and quite tall in her own right, a regal woman.

She said, "Your father warned me. Still . . . a foot. I had not realized how much taller a foot is."

"Yes, ma'am."

She hugged him. She pulled him in through the foyer, into the long, wide room he remembered from his last visit. He put down the pack and went at once to the window. Central Park had not changed; it was still green in September. He had known the park and loved it long ago when he was little.

"How is your father? And . . . Christine? That is her name, isn't it, Christine?"

"Yes, ma'am. Christine. They're the same."

12

"They cannot be the same." She had a lovely voice; she spoke distinctly and generally in full sentences. "We all change. Look how you have changed."

"Have I?" There were people in the park, small as ants. He had heard about the muggings and all the other stories but it all appeared innocent and beautiful in the afternoon sun.

"Well, my dear, barefoot sandals are not exactly what one expects in the city. And no jacket. And your hair—really son, you must get a haircut. There's a fine barber at the Pierre. You do remember the Pierre?"

"Yes, mother, I remember."

There was a small silence, then she said. "We are supposed to have a talk. Your father wrote me. Trouble, he said. You've had trouble."

He faced her, found a deep, comfortable chair, plumped down upon it and looked at her long and hard. "Always trouble, mother. They said . . . someone said that I march to a different drummer."

"A quotation, darling. People are fond of saying things like that about other people who do not quite conform."

"That's it. I don't conform."

"And he intimated that you 'do drugs.' Is that the expression, 'do drugs'?"

"I was caught smoking a joint at Armory School."

"Yes, a joint. That's marijuana." She smiled without mirth. "No more harmful than beer, I have learned."

"They caught me drinking beer at Butterly School."

"And something about a girl at Middleville?"

"Something. That was a bad number. A bum rap."

13

"Was she a nice girl?"

"There was a difference of opinion," he said. "To me, she was a nice girl."

"Your father's son," she breathed. "Of course."

Willy suddenly grinned. "He said I was my mother's son."

Now she flushed, putting a hand to her cheek. She was, after all, thirty-seven and fighting every day of it. She recovered quickly, not looking away from him. "Harper School is coeducational. I hope you'll be discreet."

"Father says it's my last chance. If I don't make good he won't have me home again." He gulped and said, "I wouldn't live here, you know that. So it's straight on."

She went to him then and put her arms around his neck and wept. "Oh, Willy, it's been so unfair, so terribly unfair. Life's been so cruel to you . . ."

There was the sound of a key in the outer door. She stiffened and reached for a fragile kerchief and dabbed at her eyes. A small man, shorter than she, entered the room. He was impeccably attired, his hair was styled, he was young-old. His name was Bosley Brevoort.

He stood a moment, then said, "Ah, Willy. I see you have made your mother weep again. So often, poor girl, so often she has wept for you."

Willy wearily arose. "Good afternoon, Mr. Brevoort. Uh—mother, I'd better go. He's too much like the other one, the one you married after you left father. I'll be in touch—just over the river, you know. G'bye."

She reached out one hand, then dropped it to her side. He shouldered the backpack and started for the door. Brevoort stepped aside, smiling, pleased.

"I wanted you to see the show tonight," his mother cried. "I wanted you to have a nice evening."

"My dinner coat went with a trunk to Harper," he said. "Just stopped by to say hello and all." He did not look again at Brevoort. He detested the man and his money and his whole long line of ancestors. The years had not made a difference. Willy went out of the apartment and down to the street.

"Cab?" asked the doorman.

"Please."

He felt a bit woozy. It was jet lag, he thought. A pleasant stewardness had chatted with him, telling him that it wasn't the time spent sitting in the plane but the pressure in the cabin that caused jet lag. He had been vaguely interested. Now he was hungry and the best thing he could do was go over to Jersey and face Harper School and whatever it held in store for him. Nothing of interest, he thought. The basketball team was lousy. Everyone prepared for Harper College, which was in Pennsylvania, an old and distinguished institution. He had read all about it in the brochures. Harper School was not all that old and it had a financial problem which his parents had helped to alleviate, he supposed. It was probably the way they had made Harper accept him.

Not that it mattered. It was the season to begin basketball practice. He could lose himself in the game whether or not the team was any good. Just so he had the outlet, so he could forget the many things he wanted to put out of his mind.

He changed to his basketball shoes in the taxi. He supposed that he had worn the sandals to irritate his mother. He was not quite certain why he did these things but it was somehow out of his control.

The bus station was crowded but he found the proper vehicle for Morristown and at the rear of the bus there was a vacant seat. He sat down, cramming his pack in the rack above, glancing at the other occupant of the leather seat. She was a tall girl. She had a lean body, long legs, and the face of an innocent child. She held herself erect, not slumping as did some of the tall girls on the West Coast. She caught him looking at her, flushed, then turned toward him. She showed him a small, cool smile.

He said, "These buses weren't built for us long-legged people, were they?"

"I have a hunch you're headed for Morristown," she replied. She had a nice, fresh voice.

"Harper School."

"Yes. They said there'd be a guard from the West. They said he was very good."

"Who said?"

"The girls. You know, the girl basketball fans."

"Oh. Are you one of them?"

She shook her head. "Tennis. I'm Pamela Stern."

"Willy Crowell."

"That's it. Willy Crowell. They say you were in some kind of trouble out there."

"They sure know a lot."

"They think they do," she assured him. "Harper's full of people who think they know all about everything and everybody."

"Well, I've been thrown out of several schools," he told

16

her. There was that about her which invited confidence. "For lots of reasons."

After a moment she said, "You don't have that look about you."

"What look?"

"Well, I've known a lot of kids who couldn't get along with . . . school . . . the teachers . . . the coaches. All that. They have a certain look."

He thought about that for a moment. There was Dingy and Fuller and Shafer and they did somehow seem to be different. He had been in trouble with them and they had been good fun—but there was a recklessness, he now realized, a flair that you could see if you recognized it. It was in their eyes, in the way they moved and the way they laughed too loud and too often.

He said, "Maybe you're right. Maybe I don't look it. But there's the record."

"Hey, this is pretty heavy," she said. The smile came and went. "Harper's all right, really. I mean, Botley's a nice man. You know, the headmaster. The faculty's good. There's a lot of stuff about Harper College and how we all should go there and make it even greater than it is. It's supposed to be one of the best small colleges in the East, you know."

"I heard." He was amazed at himself. He never spoke to strangers, seldom carried on a conversation with anyone. He felt himself retreating into his shell. He made an effort. "You on the tennis team?"

"Uh-huh."

"Hey, wait. You're Pam Stern. Wow!"

"Thank you. I think."

"You went to the finals in the nationals."

"And got swamped by that California kid. Essie Love."

"But you're only sixteen."

"So is she," said the girl moodily. "You Westerners, you play all year."

"Yeah," he said. They were silent awhile, watching the New Jersey side of the river appear, watching the blight of the city. Then they were rolling on the highway to the hills and the terrain brightened, soiled only by occasional gas stations, junk food palaces, and billboards.

He asked, "Was it tough, losing?"

"It's always tough. Don't you ever lose?"

"All the time. Not in basketball so much, though."

"It's tough," she said. "I didn't just lose. I got wiped."

"Still, the finals."

"That's what everyone tells me. It's not enough."

It was then he noticed her chin. It was rounded and pretty enough but it was also very firm. There was a beginning ridge of muscle along the jawline. He did not remember ever having looked so closely at a new acquaintance. He was faintly embarrassed.

He said, "I know what you mean. Guess it's going to be a lot of losses for the Harper basketball team, huh?"

She relaxed, grinning at him. "They were ten and twenty last year. That's why they got the new coach."

"Boots Jones. I heard about him."

"The girls say he's real strict."

"The girls seem to have the scam on just about everything."

"They stick together real good. They move around the beaches all summer and they chatter and they listen."

"Just who are these girls?"

"Oh . . . just the kids from Harper. Most of them are pretty, you know? They lead cheers, play field hockey, party a lot. You'll like them."

"I'm not much for girls." He was sorry the moment he said it. She drew away from him and stared out the window. He went on hastily. "Well, you know, they're not much for me. either." She was silent. He stumbled ahead. "What I really mean is, I hang out by myself a lot. I . . I don't even talk to people. You're . . . I never talk to people like I am now."

She relaxed a little. "They didn't tell me that."

"They don't really know about me."

"Well, sooner or later."

"Sooner or later what?"

"Harper's out in the country. People get to know each other." Now she faced him. "I'm not much around the guys, for that matter. I'm too tall."

"Not for a basketball player."

"Huh! They all go for the pretty little ones. You ought to know that."

He heard himself say, "Well, I'd like to see you . . . I mean, like I can talk to you."

"That would be nice." But she was listless, staring out at the countryside.

He had found now the place where he had always been—without words. He sensed that she too was a private person, that neither of them had the gift of easy communication. He resigned himself and looked past her at the scenery, which grew more bucolic, greener, more inviting. They came to Morristown. He said, "I guess we're here."

He stepped back and admired her as she walked, straight-

19

backed and steadily, to the front of the bus. When they had reached the ground she waited for her suitcase to be disemboweled from the bulk of the bus. He stood by, silent.

She said, "They'll be expecting us."

He then saw a four-door station wagon, chastely lettered in script, "Harper School." They entered it. The driver was a grizzled man who spoke to Pam and was introduced to Willy as "Mr. Grumman."

Mr. Grumman negotiated the heavy traffic with skill. He turned westward and northward and came to a two-lane macadam road, a thick white line in the center. He wore a well-kept jacket from one of the armed services and a blue beret. He spoke over his shoulder.

"School's mighty proud of you, Miss Stern."

"Thank you, Gus."

"You, Mr. Crowell, you're the California hotshot basketball guard, huh?"

"I'm Willy Crowell."

One shoulder lifted. "Boots Jones has been braggin' on you. You and Hoby Barker from last year. Says he'll have a winnin' team. Ha!"

Pam said, "You don't believe it, Gus?"

"I been around Harper since it opened. Since the war. That's War II, Mr. Crowell. We never had a winnin' team at nothin' until Miss Stern came to play tennis."

There seemed to be no reply to this. They had come to gently rolling hills, fine houses set far back from the road. The reds and browns of autumn were not yet on parade. The land seemed lush and fertile but uncultivated. White fences stretched near and far. There were occasional small herds of cattle, contentedly fat and well-tended.

20

Pam said, "The farms of the rich. They commute to the city when they have to. They ride to the hounds. You believe that? They ride after foxes."

"Tax write-offs," he said. "Gee, so close to New York and no vegetables or fruit or anything." It was wrong, he thought. The taxi driver had shown him the poor of New York, the way they lived. Something was wrong.

Grumman made a turn onto a narrower road which ascended still another small hill. The school sat at the top amidst elms planted a century agone. It had a certain aloofness, Willy thought, combined with dignity.

"Prettiest prep school in the country," Grumman said. "Built on the plans of Harper College over in Bucks County. Miz Harper did it. Like it's in the family. She made all the plans, everything. I sure wish she'd come home."

They stopped at an ivy-covered dormitory. Grumman managed Pam's suitcase. She stood a moment, hesitant. Then she spoke softly. "It was nice, Willy."

"Real nice." There was formality in the parting; each was wary within the hearing of Grumman. She went toward the dorm.

He watched her enter the building. There were girls at the window; they shouted greetings. Pam lifted a hand, unsmiling, going in her regal way to the entrance.

Grumman said, "You're to see the headmaster. You want me to take that whatever-you-call-it to your dorm?"

"Whatever you say."

"That's the best way. Botley, he's a stickler for dress and all. Mebbe you'd wanta spruce up?"

"No," said Willy. "I'm a bit late now."

Grumman gave him an unexpectedly shrewd glance. "Got

21

your own way 'bout you, I reckon. Westerners, they're like that. Seen a lot of 'em in the Marines."

Willy had no reply. Grumman drove him on a winding narrow road to a building set apart, terraced and turreted. It was of stone, as were all the other edifices, he saw. Harper was consciously minor Ivy League, he thought. It made no difference, he told himself. It was just another school in a more beautiful setting than he had known before.

Still, he thought, ascending wide stone steps, there had been the girl. He had never spoken so easily with a stranger.

3

HE FOUND THE OFFICE of the headmaster with ease. It was at the end of a wide hall. He entered and a lady in a brown slack suit looked at him, smiled, stood behind her desk. "You're Willy Crowell."

"Yes, ma'am."

"Willy. Not William."

"They christened me Willy."

She said, "I'm Mrs. Cross. Mr. Botley expected you on an earlier bus."

"I had to see my mother."

"But . . . you're from California." She was sharply curious.

"Yes, ma'am."

The door to the inner office opened. A man said, "Crowell, come in, please. . . . Mrs. Cross, I don't want to be disturbed."

She said, "Just as you say, Mr. Botley."

Willy entered a large office with windows on two sides. The campus stretched lushly to the south; the school buildings presented their ivy-covered walls in a rectangle. In the distance was the athletic field with wooden bleachers such as the public high schools in California sported without pride.

A lettered triangle on a large, cleared desk spelled out "T. J. Botley."

The man had sharp eyes, deep brown. His hair was receding, slicked back, not shaped in the modern manner. He had a wide mouth and a square chin. He was dressed in a tweed jacket, blue slacks, and black loafers. His shirt was open at the throat, a tie knotted loosely. It was a striped tie with the school colors, red and white.

"Sit down, Crowell. I have a letter here from your father. And a letter from your mother."

"Yes, sir."

"And I have a complete record of your previous—er—school activities."

"Yes, sir."

T. J. Botley regarded the two letters which he placed before him on the desk. "No one is to know the name of either your father or your mother. I do not find that odd. I believe I understand the circumstances."

"Yes, sir."

"Your father is a famous motion picture star."

"Yes, sir. Rex Ball."

"And your mother is an actress well-known in the theater."

"Yes, sir. But she's remarried."

"I know. In fact, your parents have tried to make clear to me the entire situation."

Willy waited.

"Er . . . what, precisely, would you say has been your difficulty in complying with the systems of the schools you have attended?"

Willy thought that over. "Lack of communication?"

"Is that your answer?"

"I can't think of another right now—off the top of my head."

"Does that mean that you do not think the schools were adequate?"

"No, sir."

"Then the lack was on your part?"

"Yes, sir."

Botley shuffled the two letters. "Yet you were a star basketball player. People—students—must have looked up to you."

"I never noticed."

Botley's eyes became even sharper. "Is it possible that you do not notice the reactions, the responses, of the people with whom you are surrounded?"

Willy hesitated. "Yes, sir, that's possible."

Botley's expression softened. "You can be happy here, Crowell. This is a good school. It's up to you. I'll be here if ever you want to talk. Right now, the coach would like to see you." He beckoned Willy to the window. "That's the gym, at the end of the campus. Since it is a bit late, would you mind seeing him now?"

"No, sir."

"You'll find your dorm and your roommate easily enough. It's a small world here at Harper."

"Thank you, sir."

Willy walked across the campus. Boys and girls glanced at him curiously. He half-waved or nodded as seemed the proper procedure. It was late afternoon and the shadows were lengthening, and again he did not know whether he was entering a new world or another such as he had encountered rather too often.

He walked into the building which housed the gymnasium. It seemed to be the old world, the one he had been into before. The odor was there—elements of sweat and wintergreen and rubbing alcohol. He pressed on to swinging doors, from within which came the familiar tap-tap of leather upon wood.

The gym was neither old or new. It was larger than some he had known, smaller than others. It had a balcony and in a corner were bucks and horses and piled mats. Above there were ropes and rings dangling, high enough not to hinder basketball activity but reminders that gym classes were part of the curriculum. There was a group of boys in jump suits and jogging outfits and jeans circling beneath a basket, taking lay-ups and jump shots in turn. There was a young man watching very closely, giving low-voiced suggestions, an ordinary young man with brown hair and brown eyes, wearing a red and white Harper jacket. Then there was, indubitably, the head coach.

Boots Jones was a giant of a man. He had long arms and legs, and a small head. His nose had been broken more than once. His mouth turned down; he was a man who seemed never to have smiled. When the doors swished behind Willy, he turned, peered. He lifted a silver whistle from the end of a glittering chain and blew into it. The action stopped; everyone froze. There was authority in the sound of that oversized whistle.

26

Willy walked toward the group in dead silence. It was an embarrassing moment, yet there were basketballs rolling about, there were people who understood the game. He saw Coach Jones pick up one of the balls and was not amazed when it came drilling at him with the speed of light. He caught it in his large hands, spun it, dribbled as he loped toward Boots Jones.

"The late Mr. Crowell, I believe?" The voice was nasal, surprisingly high, almost feminine.

"Yes, sir."

"We hear great things about you, Crowell. Are you in shape?"

"Yes, sir."

Jones did not turn his head. His eyes were fierce, challenging. He called out, "North . . . Ruman . . . Try a two-on-one with this hotshot from California."

Two players stepped forward. The others retreated, lining up, military fashion. Willy bounced the ball once. He looked at the coach, then at his new adversaries.

One of the players was about his height, but heavier. The other was taller and heavier. Willy looked at their feet, at their hands. Then he looked into their eyes, unsmiling.

The first player said, "Hey—I'm Sig Ruman."

"Uh-huh," said Willy.

The other did not speak. He wore his hair cut shorter than was the mode, his jaw was hard, his eyes wide, a gray-blue. He looked hard, tough.

Ruman said, "That's Joe North."

"Uh-huh," said Willy.

The coach said, "You can meet each other later. I want to see something from this Johnny-come-lately." He blew the whistle, shrilling to the rafters.

Willy bent his torso. The ball slapped the floor. The two players came at him, double-teaming.

Willy whipped the ball behind him, brought it between his legs, palmed, faked with his head, went to the right. Ruman was caught flat-footed. North made a move and was too late. Willy went between them and took a shot from fifteen feet. The ball slid through the net. He followed it, retrieved it.

He took it out, dribbling, swerving, pivoting. He had the grace of ballet and the sure hands of a sculptor. When the two players converged upon him he retreated. He circled, the ball a part of him always, making a pirouette when least expected. He took it in and laid it up.

The whistle blasted again. Willy held the ball. Ruman and North were staring at him. He thought North was glaring. The silence was profound.

The coach said, "You're a showboat."

Willy threw the ball twenty feet into the basket.

"All right, you look good workin' out. We'll see about you. Guard—you'll be tryin' out for point guard."

"Yes, sir," said Willy without expression.

The coach walked away, signifying that practice was ended. The assistant came to Willy and said, "Name of Holder. Get settled and be here tomorrow after registration."

"Yes, sir." He felt nothing. The head coach was a bully. If the other players were no better than Ruman and North it would be a bad year on the courts. He found Ruman beside him as he left the building.

"Hey, man. I'm your roomie."

"Okay. That's fine."

"You sure made North and me look bad."

"Sorry about that."

"North's captain. Boots, he's already got everybody runnin' like dogs. There's one other guy, Hobey Barker. He's good. He's a guard, too."

"So?"

"So we still haven't got a team."

"You mean that a team needs ten men."

"At least six. Right?"

"The bench. Got to have a bench."

"Hobey goes both ways, guard or forward. I'll be bench. And you can see I'm no star."

Willy did not answer. Ruman was a talker but he seemed a nice kid. They walked on toward a dormitory on the opposite side of the campus from the one he had seen Pam Stern enter.

"Botley brought Jones in. Mrs. Harper, she's been in Europe a couple years. She's a hell of a nice lady."

"People say that."

"It's not all that bad here. There's some great chicks."

"Uh-huh."

"You'll see. We have fun. Boots Jones'll never stop us from havin' fun."

"Fun?"

"There's Morristown. And we get weekends in New York."

"I met Pamela Stern on the bus," Willy found himself proffering.

"Pam? Great tennis. But she don't fool around, you know? All tennis and studyin' so she can get time off for the tournaments. The guys don't dig her."

They entered the dormitory. There was a corner room on the ground floor into which Ruman led the way. Willy's trunk was in a corner, the backpack atop it. It was a huge room, containing two extra-long single beds, two comfortable chairs, two desks with straight chairs, a clean thick carpet. Bookshelves lined three walls, the other was divided by a large window overlooking the campus. A door led to a bathroom.

"They do you good here, don't they?" said Willy.

"Well, this is Harper Hall. Mainly for jocks. We got a couple A students, too. Botley's all for puttin' us on the map, you know? He's got ambitions."

"He seems okay."

"Yeah. Okay. Not great but okay . . . Hey, that's your bed, that side. You mind? I lived here last year so I'm used to my own things. I mean, if it bothers you . . ."

Willy looked at him. Ruman had crinkled at the corners of his eyes. He was entirely open, uncomplicated. "Hey, whatever you say. I'll take a shower and see what they want from me before dinnertime."

Ruman said, "Right on. I'm unpacked so I'll just goof off 'til you're set."

He saluted and left the room. Willy went into the bathroom. It was ample; the showerhead had three speeds. He hadn't realized how very weary he was until now. He undressed and used all three nozzles, luxuriating in the stinging shower. He dried himself, went to his backpack and trunk and began putting away his clothing.

Just another school, he thought. Maybe a bit more interesting. Ruman did not have the look which he had pondered earlier, the wild look. He seemed like a decent person. The headmaster wasn't too bad. Coach Jones was certainly a problem, but Willy had worked under a lot of coaches. At sixteen he was full of experience.

And then there was the girl. He put his tennis racquet in a safe place. He had been practically born on a tennis court. Maybe they could have a match. Ruman had said she didn't play around with the guys. He liked the sound of that. He could not have said why, but he liked it.

4

HOBART J. BARKER drove the car into the public garage in Morristown and the proprietor came to him, grinning, wiping his hands on a dirty towel. The 1973 Pontiac Firebird shone, silver in the morning light. The driver untangled himself with some difficulty. He was dark and lean and six feet, four inches in his basketball shoes. He wore tailored slacks and a pullover cashmere sweater.

The garage man said, "Glad to see you back, Mr. Barker."

"Same old drag, Jackson."

"You want me to drive you out?"

"After I use the phone, okay?"

"Anything you say, Mr. Barker."

Hobey Barker went to the phone in the office and called long distance to Cleveland. His mother answered. He said, "Hi, mum. I made it."

"Thank goodness. The way you drive."

"Well, I did get a couple of tickets. Just speedin', though. Nothin' bad."

"Send them along. Dad'll take care of them. Are you tired out, darling?"

"No. I'm fine. Jackson'll drive me to school, bring the car back."

"It's just as well they don't allow cars on campus. You will behave yourself, won't you, darling?"

"I always do, mum."

She chuckled. "You don't get caught is what you mean, son. However, we're not complaining. Dad says hello and much love."

"Hey, I love you both."

"Hope the basketball is better this year."

"It will be. Don't worry."

"We know it means a lot to you. But it's better not to transfer this year. And you do want to go to Harper College, don't you?"

"Yeah . . . Sure. If it was good enough for dad it's too good for me."

"All right, now. Have Jackson send us the phone bill. And call when you can."

"I can always find time to call. 'Bye for now." He hung up. He stretched his limbs, which were stiff from the long ride. His folks were the best, no question about it. They must know he had stayed over in New York. They never questioned him. He went out of the office and Jackson was waiting in clean overalls. They drove out to Harper School, chatting amiably about the care of the car, which was in perfect condition despite the mileage on it, about the weather, about basketball.

"I hear the hot kid from California got in yesterday," Jackson said.

"He'd better be real hot."

"You got that new coach from the pros. Maybe you can make it this year, win some."

34

"We'll win some. That is, if Crowell's any good. Jim North and me and a real good guard can win a few."

"Just who is this California dude?"

"Don't know and don't care. Just so he's as hot as they say he is."

"I'd like to make some bets. Point spreads, y' know?"

"I'll be letting you know. You take care of the car and the other things. I'll take care of you."

"Right on, man."

At Harper Hall Jackson parked and began taking luggage from the rear seat and the limited trunk of the car. Hobey Barker went indoors, past the room assigned to Willy and Sig to the far end of the corridor. Joe North opened the door at the sound of his footsteps and they embraced one another briefly, exchanging loud greetings.

The room was even larger than the one at the front of the building. It contained a color television set, a stereo, and a small refrigerator in addition to the other furniture.

Hobey said, "Hey, man, break out the stuff."

"Right, man." Joe North went to the refrigerator and brought out two bottles of beer. Jackson came in with the bags and another bottle manifested itself like magic. The three sat down behind closed doors.

"How's it look?" asked Hobey.

"The California kid is flashy as hell, is how it looks. A real showboat."

"Is he any good?"

"Too good." **2090320**

"What's that mean?"

"He's like a pro, man. All that jazz. He won't fit in. I can smell it."

"What about the new coach?"

"I got him snowed. He made me captain." North shrugged. "If you'd been here it would've been you, I expect. Jones and Botley, they're like bugs in a rug."

"It doesn't matter," said Hobey. "Just so we have the inside. Right, Jackson?"

"Right, Mr. Barker. Hey, I gotta get back to the shop."

Hobey took out a wallet. It was comfortable with crisp new currency. He handed a bill to the garage man and said, "Keep the tab straight and all will be like forever."

"Thanks, Mr. Barker . . . Mr. North, be seein' you."

The two tall young men drank their beer, placed the empties in a paper sack to be secretly disposed of later, and sprawled in the easy chairs.

"So the new dude is fancy, huh?"

Jim said, "A workout. But he's somethin' else, looks like."

"One of us?"

"That's the trouble. Funny thing, they roomed him with Big Mouth Ruman. And he's the quiet type, this Crowell."

"Quiet?"

"One of those 'yes sir' and 'no sir' guys. You know?"

"I'll have to check him out with Mrs. Cross."

"You sure got her in your pocket."

Hobey tapped the pocket containing his wallet. "She needs. And she's nosey."

"I got to say, pal, you really know how to use that bankroll your folks lay on you."

"You'll learn."

36

"My folks don't come through like yours."

"True . . . True . . . And they have more money than do mine." Hobey helped himself to another beer. "So . . . back to basketball. How do you see it?"

"You and me at forward. Ambs at center. The new guy, Crowell, and Caponetto at guards."

"Hagen and Ruman good bench. That's about it."

"Rohm, Malone, Field, Alexander. They stuck it out last year."

"You think the coach can put it together?"

"He's a former pro. I think everyone who can cut it will get playin' time."

"Just so we know how it goes."

North frowned. "You sure we can trust Jackson? If it ever got out we were betting on the games . . ."

"If it got out we were puttin' away these beers it would be the same thing."

Joe went to the refrigerator. "Right. So here's to fun and plenty of it."

"That's the name of the game," said Hobey. "Fun. You're only young once, my folks always say."

They drank as they busied themselves putting away Hobey's considerable wardrobe. They laughed a lot at the witticisms of each other. They were having a very good time. Basketball was tomorrow and each was superbly confident of his ability. They drank beer and talked of the good times to come, the fun times.

5

PAMELA STERN roomed alone. It was the only single room in the girl's dorm, a sort of cupola under the eaves with a couple of narrow windows, sparse furniture but good light. Her family had spent a lot of money on her tennis career and she was fortunate to have a scholarship—a double scholarship for both tennis and A grades. When Marion Thompson knocked on her door she put down her copy of a tennis magazine in some surprise.

Marion was a redhead, a beautiful girl. She was the only tennis player who could give Pam a fairly decent workout. She said, "Hey, there. How are you, champ?"

"Runner-up," said Pam. "What's the scoop?"

"They want you downstairs."

"Who, me?" "Downstairs" meant the room of Kathy North, sister of Joe North, cheerleader extraordinary, campus queen.

"They just elected you housemother."

"You're putting me on."

"No, seriously. You're the one who can get to the faculty. I mean, you get the grades, you're the school heroine, all that."

"I don't need the responsibility."

"Come down and talk with us," said Marion. "You know

we're not getting any benefit from Title IX. Everything goes to the boys."

"Since when does anyone care?" Until now she had experienced trouble getting a practice court in the season.

"Kathy got a bug up her rear end this summer. She worked for ERA or something. And you know her people give money to the school."

"But Kathy doesn't do anything but bounce around leading cheers."

"I know that. You know that. Everyone knows it. But Kathy wants equal funds for field hockey and she wants girls' basketball and—oh, I don't know what all she wants."

"And I'm to be the goat?"

"Pam, you're always off by yourself. Look, I'm your friend. Take a shot at this, will you?"

"The guys don't like me as it is," Pam said. "If I start into this they'll purely hate my guts."

Marion said, "But that's just the reason . . ." She broke off. Then she said, "You never cared a hoot about the guys before now, did you?"

Pam felt the flush staining her cheeks. "Okay . . . Okay. I'll go down and listen."

"The tour must have done something to you. For you?" Marion laughed.

"Never mind." But she thought about Willy Crowell all the way downstairs.

Kathy's room, which she shared with another pretty blonde named Wanda Wills, a fellow cheerleader, was furnished exactly as was that of her brother. The North family was nothing if not impartial. Pam was immediately handed a cold glass of Perrier water and a cookie. She leaned against

40

the door and listened. Kathy North was blue-eyed and shapely. Her gaze was direct and she spoke crisply and well. She had the body all the boys admired and she wore sweaters a size too small and skirts which flared and, despite it all, she was bright in the head, Pam thought. She talked about the Equal Rights Amendment and Title IX, which proclaimed all girl athletes equal to the men. She made a good speech but there was nothing in its contents that Pam had not read in magazines or heard on the tennis circuit.

Wanda Wills, who was blonde with the aid of certain chemicals, Pam knew—and pert and lovely—was Kathy's friend and follower. With Marion, they were of the Harper School elite; they led more than cheers. The other girls liked them, believed in them.

Kathy was saying, "You've come closer than anyone to putting Harper School in the public eye, Pamela. Now is your chance to do something here, something for all of us."

"Just what sport are you going into?" Pam asked.

"Well . . . what I want is for the cheerleaders to travel with the teams. The other girls have their own things. What we want is for you to take it to the faculty. Old Botley's crazy about you."

"I haven't noticed. But I haven't met him since I came back."

"He'll be ape," said Kathy. The other girls all nodded. "He'll listen to you."

"But he won't do anything," Pam told them. "He hired a high-priced basketball coach."

"That's the point. If he can do that for the boys, let him do something for us girls."

"You have something there," Pam admitted. "But I don't like the job."

"We voted. It was unanimous."

"Uh-huh. Since we're into human rights, who made you kids boss?" asked Pam bluntly. "Last year you were into smoking pot and sipping wine and talking existentialism. Which I'm sure none of you could define. Which I'm not too sure what it means myself. Now it's women's rights. Honestly, I can see myself on a limb and you kids busily sawing it off behind me."

"Oh, no, Pam," said Marion. "No way. It's true, you have your own thing. I mean none of us has the position that you have. We know that. We won't let you down."

"You get the best grades. You're the tennis champ," Kathy said. "You don't fool around. You're perfect for the job."

"Housemother. What a rotten thing to be," Pam said. "Housemother to a bunch of kooks."

Marion laughed and after a moment they all laughed with her. Then Kathy North sobered.

"Maybe we're a bit strung out on this. Are you going to put us down?"

"No," said Pam. "I just don't want to carry the ball."

"You'll do it, though?"

Pam finished the Perrier. "I hate to, but I suppose I will. Draw up a resolution. Get your ducks in line. Then get together and talk about it."

"Great! We'll show them a thing or two." Kathy waved her cracker. "I knew we could depend on you."

"Uh-huh," said Pamela. "See you around, kids." She left the room. She could hear their voices buzzing as she departed. They had to have something, she thought. They were not stupid; they needed a cause. Any cause would do, she added, just so they kept their little minds occupied. Of them all, only Marion had common sense.

She started for the stairs, realized that she was restless. She felt stale. She had not hit a tennis ball in too long a time, she thought. She went out of the dorm and onto the campus. It was a cool evening in New Jersey and a moon was flirting with casual clouds. She walked toward the artificial lake, which was fed by streams from the hill despite having been excavated by bulldozers hired through Mrs. Harper.

She saw the tall boy before he saw her. Instinctively, she whirled around to start in the other direction. Her feet scuffed loose stones and he called out.

"Pam? Pam Stern?"

She stopped. "Is that you, Willy Crowell?"

"It isn't my brother." He came toward her, walking briskly. "Fact is, I haven't got a brother."

"Why do people say things like that? We all do."

"Because we can't think of anything else to say."

He was beside her now, towering comfortably over her. They were both wearing flat-bottomed shoes. If she wore high heels she would still not be as tall as he.

She asked, "How do you like it so far?"

"It's cool. Roomie seems okay—Sig Ruman."

"Talks a good game. He's okay. The coach?"

"Problems, I'd say."

"The headmaster hired him. Holder, the assistant, was coach last year. Holder teaches biology."

"I see. Amateur night in Dixie."

She said, "The cheerleaders just made me an offer I couldn't turn down—though I wanted to." She told him about it.

He listened without comment.

She said, "I'm already unpopular. This'll do it."

He looked at her in the moonlight. Her face seemed more mature than he had thought on the bus that afternoon. "You care about that?"

"A little. Doesn't everybody?"

"I never did."

"Well, when you have goals . . ." She broke off.

"Like you want to be world champion?"

"And go to college and do something with my life. Yes."

He thought it over. "Most girls just want to get married and have kids and be rich. Leastways that's how it seems."

"That's what women's rights is all about."

"Is it? I wouldn't know."

"You want to go into pro basketball?"

"Nope."

"Then what?"

He did not answer for several seconds.

"Don't you know?" she asked.

"No. Not yet."

They walked. The cicadas buzzed, the tree frogs in the elms harrumphed. A bulky figure appeared, doggedly jogging toward them. Willy instinctively stepped forward as if to meet a challenge. The big man slowed. His face was sweaty, his jaw tight.

He said, "Crowell?"

"Yes, sir, coach."

44

Boots Jones asked, "What are you doin' out here walkin' with a girl? You should be runnin', stayin' in shape."

"This is Pamela Stern. Coach Jones." Willy was calm, even amused. "We both stay in shape."

Jones wiped an arm of his jogging jacket across his brow. "Pam Stern? Pleased to meet you. Maybe you both should be runnin'."

"I have my own training notions," Pam said primly.

The coach suddenly grinned. "Well, why not try it that you run and he chases you?" Then he went past them, trotting toward the school buildings.

Pam said, "At least he's got a sense of humor."

"Surprise, surprise."

"There's something about him. Tough but . . . something."

"Just plain tough," said Willy.

"He was a pro."

"And you'll be a pro next year. Right?"

"When I graduate."

"Lots of money in tennis."

"Lots of money in pro basketball but you're not interested. Don't you care about the game?"

"Care about it? Why—it's all I care about. I mean, that's my thing. That's what I do best."

"What about classes, studies?"

"I do all right."

They came to the head of the lake. They could hear the cold water burbling down from the distant hills. The clouds went flying before a wind and the moon threw light upon them. They paused a moment. It was a beautiful evening.

45

The stars began to show, one by one.

She said, "I think you're a strange one, Willy Crowell."

"That's what they all say."

"Maybe we're both strange."

"Maybe we should kind of—uh—see about that."

"How's your tennis?"

Now he laughed. "I was going to ask you if you wanted to work out some day when I'm not practicing too late."

"You're not afraid of being beaten by a girl?"

"That'll be the day," he promised her.

"Oh, I forgot. You're a Californian."

"Never was whipped by a girl. Played a few of 'em, too."

"It'll be fun," she said. "Shall we go back?"

"Reckon we should."

They had little or nothing to say all the way back to the campus. It seemed to them that they did not need to talk much more that evening. He saw her to her dorm and left her. She went up to her room, closed the door, and sat down in her deep chair. It was the first time she had ever talked seriously with a boy since she was twelve, she thought. Of course it had to be a laconic, oddball type. There was something wrong, something missing from him. It could be a challenge. It could be trouble. It could be quite a number of things.

What with one thing and another, she told herself, her senior year at Harper could be just about anything she wanted to make it. For the first time outside the limits of her tennis career she felt a pulse stirring, anticipation of events to come.

46

6

IT WAS RAINING, a light autumn fall. Sig Ruman grumbled all the way to the gym but to Willy it seemed fresh and good. In California it never rained but it poured. He could smell the freshness of the lingering green of September. They were early for practice.

In the locker room they changed to warm-up clothing. They were ready when Joe North entered with Hobey Barker.

Sig Ruman said, "Hey, men. Hobey Barker, this is Willy Crowell."

Barker said, "Hi." The handshake was almost a contest. Willy held firm, then relaxed. Barker stepped back and they measured one another.

It was, Willy recognized with a sigh, instant apathy. Barker was poised, handsome, the epitome of the young athlete. He was too perfect. He also carried an invisible chip on his shoulder. Willy had no desire to knock it off.

Sig rattled on, "Guess you two cats will do it, huh? Looks good, mighty fine. Caponetto's safe; he's tough. It'll be me ridin' the bench. But if I can be the sixth man, that'll be fine with me."

"Sixth man is big," said North. "Sixth man is mighty important."

"After last year . . . the pits," said Sig. "What the hell, a winnin' season. It'd be terrific, huh?"

"Like a miracle," said Barker.

From behind the lockers the voice of Boots Jones demanded, "Who said that?"

He appeared. He wore the basketball uniform of the Los Angeles Lakers. The purple and gold was slightly faded. He had long, rippling muscles and his slight paunch was hard. "You, Barker? Hear me, miracles do happen. We make 'em happen. Now get out there and take those stretchin' exercises. Never begin work without stretchin'. And get those girls outa there."

"Gee, coach," said Sig. "They're allowed."

"Cheerleaders," said Barker. "Who needs them?"

"Everybody needs 'em," said Jones. "But get rid of them now." He left abruptly as Holder came in view, paused, then accompanied him as they went to his office.

Sig said, "Hey, I'm not tellin' Kathy and them anything."

North and Barker showed no sign of moving. Willy went slowly into the gymnasium. Two blondes and a redhead were doing a dance step to softly playing music from a recorder. Pam Stern sat on the players' bench, watching. The girls were performing very well, Willy thought. He had watched the California champions for years and these kids were right up there, bright and shiny. He looked at the bench, felt instant relief. Something about Pam Stern seemed to give him confidence.

He watched for another moment or two, then sauntered to where Pam sat. She looked up at him and frowned. He sat down beside her.

48

He said, "Hey, how are you today?"

She maintained a deadpan and said, "We must stop meeting like this."

"My territory," he pointed out. "Coach wants the floor. Can you handle it?"

"You mean without getting static?"

"You know how it is."

She looked at her wristwatch. "They have five more minutes."

"Well, it'll take that much time to get the squad organized, I guess." He relaxed beside her. Sig Ruman peered out the locker room door, was relieved, came to sit with them. At that moment Coach Jones and Holder appeared at the far end of the gym.

Jones bellowed, "I thought I told you kids to get the girls out of here."

Pam arose to her considerable height. Her voice was full and loud. "When their time is up they will leave, Mr. Jones. And please do not yell at us."

Jones stopped in his tracks. He looked hard at Pam. He turned on his heel and went back into his office. Holder grinned and continued into the gym.

Willy said, "Oh, boy. Jonesy's going to call the headmaster. Seems to me I've heard this song before."

"Where?" asked Sid.

"Every place I been," said Willy.

The music ran down. Kathy, Wanda, Kitty Wheeler, a dark beauty, and Marion came, flushed with their efforts, to Pam Stern. Kathy was obviously furious.

"Now's the time, Pam," she said. "You go right over and talk to Botley and raise hell."

"Such language," murmured Sig. "You gals startin' a revolution or something?"

Pam said, "Take it easy, Kathy. Let the steam go down. I'll be there."

"It's your job!"

"I said I'd be there." Pam winked at Willy, arose and walked out of the gym with her customary dignity.

Kathy wheeled on the two boys. "You'll learn. We're going to get our rights. You'll see."

She led the others out of the gymnasium, heads high, skirts swirling.

Sig asked, "Now what the who?"

The assistant coach said, "Women's lib. Okay, boys. Let's get to stretching those ligaments."

The rest of the squad was straggling onto the court. Holder lined them up and began giving them the cadence. Willy knew about stretching; he had been through it all. He also realized the value of loosening ligaments and muscles before trying quick starts and pivots. He was well into it when Coach Jones came to him at the end of the line and tapped him on the shoulder.

Willy paused and asked, "Yes, sir?"

"You know about those gals? What they're up to?"

"Not my bag," Willy told him, meeting his eyes squarely, without expression, steady.

"Well . . . Somethin's up . . . Anyway, I want you and Caponetto to start working out defense and bringing the ball downcourt. North and Barker are the shooters up front. Get the ball to them when you can. Otherwise, take your shots. You know what I mean, take your shots?"

"Yes, sir."

"I mean, you're probably a hell of a shot. So, you take 'em. Caponetto, he's not that good. He's quick and smart and a passer. I use the press. Man-to-man or full court. I use the pro press. You understand that?"

"Yes, sir."

"California." He tapped his chest. "The Lakers. UCLA. I been there, Crowell. That's basketball. I don't know if these kids can manage it. They never did. You dig?"

"Yes, sir."

"You don't talk much, do you, Crowell?"

"No, sir."

"Well, get with North, Barker, Ambs, Caponetto. I'll line up the others. Understand there's nobody got a job sewed up, not even North and he's captain."

"Yes, sir."

Jones stared at him. "Sometimes you're aggravatin', you know that, Crowell? I hope you're as good as your record says."

Willy saw no sense in replying to this. He was undergoing a certain melancholy. He had heard so much so often from coaches and it had all come to so little that the words seemed to cascade into one ear and out the other, hard as he might try to retain them.

Holder had finished his stretching routine. Jones blew on the loud whistle and went through a pep speech. Again it was all too familiar to Willy. He found himself regarding his fellow guard, Al Caponetto.

"I'm from Newark," Caponetto said.

He was six feet tall and looked as if he belonged on a football field. His muscles were developed like those of a weight lifter. He had round brown eyes and a white-toothed grin.

"How come this team did so bad last year?"

"We play Newark teams sometimes."

"I see," said Willy.

The coach was saying, "All right, you guys stay down at this end of the court and start getting acquainted. Pass, shoot, move. I want everybody movin' with or without the ball. Remember that. It's rule numero uno. Move!"

A skinny, tall boy brought out a bag of basketballs and spilled them on the court. Holder went down to the other end with the remainder of the squad. Willy snapped a ball into his grasp and passed it to Caponetto, who gave it to North, who flipped it to Barker, who shot from underneath with great style. The center, Ambs, provided the post, a six-six, gangling lad with wide shoulders and long arms. They looked to Willy to be good enough for prep or high school competition anywhere in the country.

It was awhile before he noticed that the pattern of play was attuned to North and Barker. It was the two who dominated, alternating in setting each other up for a shot at the basket. Caponetto was into it, as was Ambs. It was, he recognized, a habit developed from previous seasons.

The next time he got the ball he faked the pass, dribbled with the speed of an antelope, and went in for a lay-up. He went back to position, silent, awaiting the reaction.

It came from North. "Showboating, Crowell?"

Willy shrugged. "Defense is right on. But you need a shooter from outside or in, someone to try the back door."

"And you're the coach?" demanded Barker.

The voice of Boots Jones thundered. "Crowell is right. We'll get around to that later. I wanta see everybody take

52

shots. Nobody's feedin' the forwards, not in my style."

North, the ball in his hands, said, "That's the way we were taught, Coach. That's our game."

Jones was on him like a mountain lion attacking a rabbit. "Your game? You loser, you're talkin' about your game? Are you out of your skull? You play my game, captain, or you sit on the bench."

The absolute force of the attack left North speechless. Hobey Barker opened his mouth, then shut it tight. Caponetto grinned at Willy. Ambs flexed his long arms, picked up a loose ball and from twenty feet out deposited it through the hoop.

Jones said, "Now let's see it, a varied attack, more movement, lots of movement without the ball." He went back down with Holder and the other players.

North said, "Aw, the hell with that. We've got our own style. How are we going to pick up his game in two weeks?"

Caponetto said, "Might try workin' on it."

"Yeah," said Ambs. "He's the boss."

Barker seemed a bit aloof. When the rotation began again he was meticulous in his action. He was truly fluid, Willy saw. He could make all the moves. If he did manage to get most of the shots, he was at least good at making them. Caponetto was strong; he would make a good cop. Every successful team had an enforcer to prevent domination under the boards or in tight spots by the opposition. Ambs was tall enough, if a bit slow. He was a boy who had grown too swiftly, Willy thought, whose future was bright.

Becoming interested in his own analysis, he increased his pace, setting up sharper passes, darting to position for picks

53

and blocks, pushing himself. The others responded. The ball went around and up into the basket and down and around with speed and aplomb.

And then he noted that the action slowed down. He knew at once that it was North and Barker who were the cause. They were not in top condition, he thought. He could smell the sweat on them, could see their knees tremble.

The unmistakable whistle of the coach sounded. They turned to him. Holder had his group together and was talking earnestly to them.

Jones said, "All right. I want to see a scrimmage. I want to see you all go against each other. Remember what I said. No man's job is safe on my team. Ambs, come here and jump off against Rohm. The rest of you take your positions and get into it. This is for real . . . I want action!"

North muttered to Barker, "Jeez, this guy never stops workin' you."

Caponetto came close to Willy and said, "Beer don't make it."

"I thought I saw a letdown in there."

"You drink?"

"Sometimes."

"You smoke?"

That did not mean regular cigarettes, Willy knew. "I have."

"But you're a jock first?"

"Right now, yes."

Caponetto nodded, satisfied. "Let's show these jerks."

They took their places. Ace Rohm, center, was all elbows and knees, as tall as Ambs. Fred Hagen was the epitome of the normal basketballer, technically right but without inspi-

54

ration. Trix Field followed the action as Sig Ruman assumed a position opposite Willy.

Sig said, "Here goes. I gotta be sixth man."

"Take your best shot," Willy told him.

Jones stood on the sideline. Holder threw up the ball. Ambs easily got the tap and went back to North with the ball. Willy took off down the lane, faking and changing speed. He was clear within fifteen feet. He stopped, knowing he had beaten Sig.

North held the ball, looking for Barker. Ambs went into the high post.

Danny Malone, the second-string guard, stole the ball cleanly. He gave to Hagen who took it down. Willy drove across court but ran into a block by Rohm. The call went to Sig, who laid it up for the score.

The whistle shrilled. "North! What the hell were you doin', playin' Statue of Liberty? Didn't you see that Crowell was open and waitin'?"

"He was outside," said North. He was panting a little. "I wanted to give it to Hobey inside."

"What you want and how the game is played seem to be two horses in different stables," said Jones. "You get the ball to the open man. You get that? To the open man."

"But Hobey never misses inside," North insisted.

Jones stared at him. North stared back.

The coach said, "You want to play my game or yours?"

There was a moment of dead silence. The captain at Harper School was the leader, Willy recognized. It was an old tradition, one that imposed an impossible condition on a strong coach.

Jones said, "Field, in for North. In my office, North."

The captain and the coach walked the length of the gym. Holder took the ball to center court. Ambs faced off against Rohm. Then when the action began, Willy made his move, the ball in his control. He dribbled past the astounded second team, came down to the key. He shot without effort and scored.

Holder blew his whistle. He said, "Nice work, Crowell. But where was the rest of the team?"

Nobody replied. They went back to work.

It was uneven. Willy passed off twice to Barker, who took long shots and missed. Barker never passed the ball to Willy.

It was going to be that kind of a situation, Willy thought. It did not affect his play. It scarcely affected his mind. He had been through it all before. It took time to sink into the heads of strangers that he was an exceptional basketball player. It took more time to overcome the ego, the petty jealousies of certain young men. He played his game unselfishly but did not expect a return in kind.

He became aware that the coach and North had returned and were on the sideline. The tap went to Caponetto who promptly gave it to Willy. Ambs was downcourt, covered by Rohm. Willy found an opening, shot through, drew Rohm's attention, passed to Ambs, who scored.

The whistle shrilled. Jones said, "North, in for Field. Caponetto, that was sound. Crowell, your pass was good. Now let's see more teamwork. And more movement, all of you."

North's face was flushed. He took his place as they faced off. The fall went to Willy, who gave it to North in the corner. North was covered by Hagen. He swiveled and Willy came in a circle, dodging Ruman. North gave him the ball. Willy faked his roommate into a pretzel and scored.

The coach had made a point, Willy thought. How it would work in the long run was another matter. Neither North nor Barker were in top physical shape, he had found. He went on at top speed, the only way he ever played the game.

The end of Mrs. Cross's rather long nose twitched with curiosity. "I can't imagine what is so important that I cannot handle it, Miss Stern."

Pam sat in the outer office of the headmaster and smiled. "Sorry, Mrs. Cross."

"Mr. Botley is very busy with registrations."

"There are no classes as yet. I can wait."

A buzzer sounded. Mrs. Cross spoke into an intercom. She looked hard at Pam and said, "You may go in now."

Botley was on his feet. He extended a hand and said, "Welcome back to Harper, Pam."

"Thank you." She took the chair he indicated. "There are a couple of matters I'd like to take up with you."

He sat down. "That sounds a bit ominous. What can I do for you?"

It was a difficult role for her. She spoke carefully. "The girls have formed a committee. I'm the spokeswoman."

His eyebrows popped. "Spokeswoman? Pam, you're a six-teen-year-old girl."

Resentment aided her. "Who has been on the tennis tour. One grows up. We have complaints and I know they're right."

57

He sighed. "Harper School simply does not have the funds for a full athletic program for girls. We do not even have funds for a football team as yet, my dear. What is it, girls' basketball, perhaps?"

"Not at the moment."

"Do you need tennis paraphernalia?"

"No. What we want is equal time on the gymnasium floor. The cheerleaders want respect. The field hocky team needs minor aid, a bit of money, more practice. We want to be recognized as equal to the boys."

"But you are equal to the boys."

"Then how can Coach Jones order us out of the gym? Why aren't we allowed full privileges?"

He thought about it for a moment. He said, "Pam, you have to consider the facts. We are not financially well off. There are many fewer girls in attendance than there are boys. We hope this season to have a representative basketball team that could improve our situation."

"You imported Coach Jones. You accepted Crowell, all the way from California because he is a star . . ."

"Crowell is qualified. His grades are good."

"And he's a star player."

"But should that prevent him from attending Harper?"

She felt slightly confused. "Aren't we getting away from the subject?"

"You brought it up."

She was no match for him, she knew. She said doggedly, "I still say the girls should be in all ways equal to the boys. If you want cheerleaders for your teams, they should have extra time to practice. They should travel with the team. That's just a start."

"They shall have it," he promised. "Is everything all right with you, Pam? You're one of our assets, you know. Anything I can do for you personally?"

"I am content. Well, maybe a little more time to work out. The courts are in terrible condition."

"There's a club in Morristown," he said slowly. "I wonder. Perhaps we can arrange something. Someone to work out with you."

She said impulsively, "Willy Crowell offered . . ." She broke off, then added, "Well, he has basketball. It'll take all of his time, I expect."

Botley smiled. "We'll work out something. And thank you for coming in, Pam."

She was dismissed. She arose, hesitated. She tried hard to think of something more to say. She felt a bit empty. She said, "Thank you for listening."

She went out past Mrs. Cross, who glared at her. She went across the campus. She wondered how to make a report to the girls. Botley had really promised nothing excepting extra time for cheerleaders. She felt she had failed.

7

THE TWO WEEKS FLED by on the wings of endeavor. Willy found the classwork surprisingly interesting. The teachers were firm but polite; they gave the work out with judgment. He had always been a good student when he was involved and the faculty of Harper School had been chosen for the purpose of involving the students, he found.

The final class on Friday was in biology. Bill Holder was the teacher. Willy was dissecting a frog. He was intent upon the delicate task when he realized the assistant coach was standing behind him.

Holder said, "You have good hands, Willy."

He held them up. "Meat hooks?"

"Good for basketball, but also for that which you are doing. You know that several pro basketball and football players turned to dentistry or surgery."

"I wouldn't want to look down throats all day." He had found he could talk easily with Holder.

"Think of surgery."

"That's a heavy think."

"Worth a try."

Holder moved on, calling back, "We leave early for Newark, you know."

They were opening the season with two games against

Central High in the nearby city. All week Willy had been hearing fearful tales about the muscle and the skill of the all-black team. He saw Pam moving closer to him.

She said, "Surgery, is it?"

"Eavesdropper."

"Those hands would look good wrapped around a tennis racquet."

"Hey, I really want to work out with you."

"I know. Basketball."

"How about Sunday morning?"

"You're playing Central on Saturday night."

"I'll be alive Sunday."

"You haven't seen a Central High team."

He said, "Pam, just between you and me and the lamp-post, I played against the pros last summer in L.A."

"Is that legal? I mean amateur?"

"Yes. It's a league for workouts. No money involved. Would you believe Dr. J. and Kareem?"

She said, "If you survived that I'll accept the Sunday morning date."

"Of course they *did* kill me."

"Of course." She went back to her frog.

It was astounding how easy it was to talk with her. He had known a lot of girls but never had he been able to carry on sensible dialogue with them. It was into the Pacific Ocean or out on the freeways to a disco or necking on Mulholland Drive or wherever a private spot could be found. This one was different.

The bell ending the day's classwork sounded softly, without the loud jangle of other schools. Willy went to his room and picked up his duffel bag. Sig Ruman had already departed for the bus.

There were three buses when Willy arrived on the scene. They were lined up before the gym and students with red and white flags and pompons were climbing into them. The team bus was painted with the same colors. Coach Jones was counting heads as the players entered it.

Willy climbed aboard. Pam had prevailed. In the rear were the cheerleaders—Kathy, Wanda, Marion, and the girl named Kitty Wheeler. They looked mighty pretty in their abbreviated skirts and tight sweaters and soft kid boots. Boots Jones glared at them, but the players seemed to accept them with equanimity if not with genuine pleasure.

The coach growled, "We oughta be talkin' game plan and here are these dames."

"Chicks," said Sig. "Dames—that's archaic, coach."

"Females." He plumped himself down behind the driver. "Let's get goin'. At least it's nearby."

They drove down the highway. The buses behind them followed closely, gay with waving flags. In the team bus Kathy North led the cheerleaders in melody, saving the cheers for later.

Willy stretched his long legs and relaxed. The team was not ready for the opposition if what he had heard about Central High was anywhere near correct. North and Barker had not yet achieved top condition and the bench was just beginning to learn the coach's full-court press. Not that it mattered. Central was not in the Jersey Conference, for some reason unknown to him. Nobody seemed to believe that Harper could give them a good game, much less beat them. He was never able to understand that feeling. He always believed that a well-coached team had a chance to win. He had never been able to enter a contest expecting to lose.

As the bus pulled out of the school grounds it passed the tennis courts. There on the bang board, stroking like an automaton, was Pam Stern. She did not turn her head, so intent was she on her work. Willy craned his neck to admire her footwork until the bus turned a corner and she was lost to view.

The short ride to Newark was uneventful. Sig Ruman said, "This town is the pits."

"It wasn't always," said Caponetto. "My father remembers when it was a nice little city."

"Long before my time," said Sig. "There's a swell library and museum and a couple of good new colleges. The rest is disasterville."

They came to the high school. It had been built sixty years before. It had broad steps, now cracked and worn by the feet of thousands of students. The way into the gym was narrow and dim. It was the most rickety building Willy had ever played in, he realized.

They dressed and went out into the gym. It was a revelation. It had been rebuilt, there was a balcony, there were temporary stands filled with strong-lunged rooters who screamed so that the rafters pealed with the echo. Some of the things Willy overheard reminded him of the pro games he had seen. They were, to say the least, impolite. In fact, they were profane. His blood began to stir.

Sig asked, "How do you like the snake pit?"

"It's the snakes that gig me," said Willy.

The Harper players were being presented. Jeers greeted each and every one and when Willy's turn came he heard a chorus that went, "California, here you go, back where grapes and oranges grow . . ." He bowed right and left and they shouted at him until the building shook as if an earthquake had followed him east.

On the bench Boots Jones told them, "So you've played here before. So they tell me this is a five-man team, that they need no substitutes. Well, I got my own notion. Go out there and run. Run like hell all the way."

Willy looked them over from across the court. Carter and Jelly were the guards, Washington and Brock the forwards; Brown was at center. They were all well over six feet tall. Brown was close to seven feet. They did not look as if they could be run off the court.

The Harper cheerleaders pranced on in their sweaters and short skirts, jiggling their pompons. The Harper contingent valorously tried to match the noise of the Central fans. They failed but, oddly, the home crowd listened without attempting to drown them out. When the girls trouped off they applauded.

Willy said, "Those cats are not all bad."

"They love the gals. It's us they hate," Sig replied.

Time was called. Willy took the court and found himself opposite Brock, who held out a huge hand and said, "Hey, California man, sorry about this, your first game and all."

Willy gave him the fraternal grip, palms up. "Right on, man from Jersey."

"Hey, you dig?"

"I dig."

"Then go, man, go."

65

The whistle sounded, the ball went up from the hands of the referee. Ambs jumped his highest but was no match for the giant Brown. Brock made a deceptive move.

Willy's mind was working automatically. He flew in front of Brock. The ball came back; both reached for it. Willy tipped it away and Caponetto seized it. Willy never paused, flying down the lane. Caponetto bounce-passed beneath Jelly's arm to Barker.

Barker passed to North and went under the basket. Willy stayed on the sideline. He was open for a moment, then the Central team collapsed in the lane. Ambs struggled with Brown. North was double-teamed. Willy made a fake right, then came in left.

North passed back to Barker. He shot. He missed. Willy was up in the air as the ball hit the rim. He took it from the reach of Brown and tipped through the hoop.

The Harper fans roared. The Central fans hooted. A small jazz band sounded a fanfare. Willy was already running toward the Harper basket, anticipating a fast break.

The ball came down, a long pass to Brock, a short cross-court pass to Alexander as Carter and Jelly closed in and Brown assumed the post. The Harper team mixed in, every player blocking, moving with his man. The ball went high to Brown who half-turned and threw a sky-hook. It went into the net and the score was even at two points.

Willy put it in play from the end line and Caponetto took it down under a full-court press. Willy checked at center court and drove for the opposite lane. Brock was on him all the way. Caponetto gave him the ball and immediately he was double-teamed. It had not taken Central long to find out about him, Willy thought. He rotated and Barker was open. He bounced the ball low.

Barker took a step and was blocked. He passed to North. North was blocked. He went for the basket. Willy moved into position in case of a miss. Brock held him as he turned. The whistle sounded.

Willy went for his foul shots. He looked at the basket, then flipped it in, bounced the ball twice upon its return to him, scored once more. It was Harper 4, Central 2.

The crowd noise had lessened; now it soared again. The swift Jelly was going down. All the Centrals ran like madmen. The Harpers also ran. The Centrals won, Brock scoring before Willy could shake a pick by Washington.

The play continued, swift and clean. There were few fouls. The Centrals ran and the Harpers ran. The count mounted to 14 all, with Willy scoring all but four of the Harper points.

Then Central began to pull away. Willy knew the reason. So did Boots Jones, who called a time-out. The team went to the bench. North and Barker stood with hands on knees, heads bent, breathing hard.

Jones said coldly, "Twenty to fourteen. And climbing. Ruman, Maloney, in at forward. Rohm take a spell at center."

North said impulsively, "Now wait, Coach."

"You heard me!" To the subs he said, "Run 'em!"

They took the court. They ran. Sig got loose and Willy passed to him, crisscrossed, tied up Brock. Sig gave him the ball. Willy scored with ease.

Central got it back but not without a struggle. The fresh Harper men fought them to a standstill. They were outclassed but not outgamed—nor outrun. The scoring slowed down. Willy came in under his own basket and stole a missed shot by Rohm by outleaping the huge Brown. He got clear, one-handed a hook and scored.

As they ran down, Brock said to him, "California man, you could almost make our team." Then Brock scored again.

Willy did not answer, saving his breath. He had not ceased running on the hard boards since the game began. Still, he did not feel particularly tired. His wind was always sound. He went step for step with Brock, made his move, shot from twenty feet out and made the basket. Still, at the half Central led by six.

Kathy and the girls came running out. As they passed the team they gave a short "Harper one, Harper two, All of us are here for you" yell. Kathy slapped Willy's shoulder and added, "You're the greatest, Crowell."

He was not truly thrilled. It had happened to him before in far places. He went into the dressing room and showered in a trickle of cold water, then changed uniforms.

Boots Jones was talking. "You're doin' good against them. If we had better condition we'd do more." He stared at North and then at Barker. "You two got your breath back yet?"

They looked straight ahead, not answering.

"Insulted because I sat you down, huh?" roared the coach. "You saw the subs do better. You saw Crowell stay with those fast cats all the way. You saw Cappy run with 'em. . . . All right, Ambs, you're big, you got an excuse and anyway you did good. You start, and North and Barker and Ruman and Crowell. Cappy, you take a rest for a few minutes. We'll talk on the bench."

Caponetto said mildly, "I'm okay, Coach."

"You're real good but we'll talk," said Jones significantly. "Now, you guys, just keep that presss on, keep pushin' 'em. Take your shots. Pass to the open man. Watch Crowell alla time."

North and Barker snorted. No one else made a sound. Jones stared at the two veterans. Then he shrugged and lifted a hand. "Stretch your muscles. Loosen up. Be ready to go-go-Go."

As Captain North led out the others Jones detained Willy. "You follow what I'm tryin' to do?"

"Keep it close, make them play their five men all the way. Then go after them tomorrow."

Jones said, "I thought you'd figure it. What about you?"

"What about me?"

"Can you last through it?"

"Yes, sir."

"Okay. Go on out there." His voice was gruff but there was a shine in his eyes. He had been a good pro basketballer. He knew talent and condition. He also knew about temperament. He frowned, following Willy, thinking of North and Barker.

Kathy, Wanda, Marion, and Kitty were lined up as Willy appeared a bit later than the rest of the squad. They were calling his name. He smiled vaguely at them, his mind on what was going to happen in the game. As he reached the bench the Central High rooters all jumped up and yelled, "California! California! Don't go! Don't go!"

He caught the sour glances of North and Barker. He raised one hand to acknowledge the cheer, then sat down, trying to make himself inconspicuous. He had scored twenty of his team's thirty points, had defended as best he could against the big, graceful, clever Centrals. So far as he was concerned he had played his regular game.

But he also knew that Barker and North were not passing off to him. Time and again he had been open and they had failed to see him. He wondered how long Coach Jones was going to put up with this or if he had no choice. He told himself it did not matter, that he did not care. The game was what mattered. He and Sig were working well and Caponetto was a fine guard with whom to play. Ambs was steady, sometimes brilliant. The other subs gave all they had at all times. Only the captain and the star seemed not to be able or willing to be a part of the whole.

Brock greeted him with the brother-handshake and said, "Hey, why did it have to be you and me?"

"Thanks."

"Y' see, our people love good basketball. That's why all the hullabaloo. You dig?"

Willy nodded. "I appreciate."

"We go all the way. You go all the way. You got a couple kids feel the same way."

"Yeah."

"That's right. No badmouthin' your own guys. Hey, where you goin' to college?"

"Harper," he said mechanically.

"I'm an A student. Put in a word for me?"

"My word wouldn't go down."

"Oho! Like that, huh?"

The referee was coming out with the ball and his whistle. The stands were chanting and stomping. Willy winked at Brock and said, "See you later."

70

It was the friendliest conversation he had enjoyed, excepting only those with Pam and Sig, he thought. Brock covered him like a blanket when the game was on but in him was a friendship, honesty—and brains. It made Willy feel very good.

The game began with Brown easily getting the tap. Willy covered Brock. The ball went to Jelly. Downcourt flowed the Centrals. Brock slipped away as Brown set a pick on Willy. He scored.

Caponetto came into the game. Willy inbounded to him. They went down the court, even North and Barker running hard. Cappy passed to Willy, who passed to North, who passed to Barker. Willy blocked Brock and Barker had a layup and the score again became a six-point margin for Central.

North and Barker were playing their hearts out now, Willy observed. Their pride was hurt. They resented Willy. They did everything right; they even passed to him when he was not in scoring position. But they kept to their own practice of feeding each other whenever possible.

The Centrals caught on and took advantage. Barker missed a shot, Brown took the rebound, Brock was downcourt like a flash to receive the pass. In a jiffy the Centrals were eight points ahead. Coach Jones asked for time.

At the bench he said, "Now hear this: The next time Crowell is open and he don't get the pass, someone comes out of the game. And that someone stays out. You hear me?"

North said, "I didn't see him open."

"Me neither," said Barker. "We're used to playing together. That's why we pass like we do."

71

Jones said, "That, gentlemen, is what I have been trying to teach you *not* to do. You heard me."

They went back into the contest. They inbounded and Willy had the ball. He saw a small opening. He dribbled into it. He saw Ambs looming. He went past Ambs, then shot a bullet pass high to the center. Ambs took it and dropped it into the hoop.

It was back to the six-point margin but Central had the ball. They flocked like antelopes down to the basket. Willy went in ahead of them. He worked around the lane, forcing big Brown to move out. He got his hands in just as Washington was passing to Brock for a setup.

Cappy grabbed the loose ball. Willy was already gone with the wind, flying along the black line. Brock was with him step for step. Cappy heaved a long one to North.

North looked for Barker, who was heavily guarded by Carter. North pivoted with the ball. Willy was working on Brock. North turned and shot. The ball fell through. Barker let out a yell, "Attaboy, Captain."

Jones called time again. He stared hard at Barker. "You sit it out."

"What? Didn't Joe score? What's wrong with that?"

"Crowell was wide open."

"Hell, what difference who makes the basket?"

"Maybe you'll learn some day," said Jones. "Sit down!"

Barker sat down. Ruman came in. The ball rambled down to the Central basket and they scored again. Sig passed in to Willy, who took it down with Brock harassing him. At midcourt he stopped dead and switched hands. Brock fell for it. Willy went back right-handed and there was Sig in the corner. Willy gave Sig the ball and into the strings it went.

Still, there was the four points difference. Willy ran down into the offense of the Centrals. Washington was passing to Brock, who went to Carter, who went to Jelly. Brown was on the high post.

Willy waited, watched. They were setting up a play. He thought about it, then seemed to desert the defensive alignment. As he did so Brock was handing off to Jelly.

Willy stole the ball. He swiveled and dribbled. He left the startled Centrals flat-footed, going in for an undefended, easy lay-up. The difference was down to two points.

It stuck there. Several fouls were called, some made, some missed. The action was furious. The Centrals, playing with their five men, were invincible. They held tenaciously to their lead.

And Barker sat on the bench. Sig Ruman seemed to improve with every minute of action. His work with Willy was pure basketball. Willy had the ball in midcourt with the clock running out. He fired. He missed.

The horn sounded. The game was over. The Central players rushed to shake hands. They had been held to a two-point victory by a team they had outclassed the previous year. They were more than friendly.

Brock said to Willy. "Tonight we sleep. Tomorrow morning?"

"Be up early. How do I find you?"

"I find you," said Brock. "Breakfast."

Kathy and the girls were treating the game as a victory. People crowded around—Harper students, Dean Botley, Holder, who had been quiet as a church mouse during the game, all the boys and girls. It was difficult to make way to a tepid shower and a change of clothing.

Barker was the first to be dressed. He waited for North, glowering, refusing to speak. Jones beckoned him aside. No one heard what was said but obviously it did not set well with the former star forward and shooter of the Harper team.

The man was needed, Willy knew. Sig was fine but the team also needed that sixth man, the key man in tough spots. Sig couldn't handle both assignments and Barker certainly would quit if he were benched. It would not be a glorious season. In fact, he wondered what would happen tomorrow against this splendid Central High team.

8

THEY WERE HOUSED in a north end motel, one which allowed Harper School to put two people in a room with twin beds for the price of a single. The curfew was, because of the night game, twelve o'clock. They were to play Central again at two in the afternoon.

The food was mediocre but they ate with the appetites of the young. Joe North and Hobey Barker went to their room and waited, talking together.

Hobey said, "That miserable coach. That stinker."

"He sure hasn't got any respect for the captain."

"He's got no respect for anybody. He's a bully and a rat."

Joe said, "I got to admit all that running made me tired."

"So what? So we went into a stall last year and got back our wind. This full-court press, what did it get us against Central?"

"They're faster than we are."

"Okay. But with a stall we might have a chance. That damn Californian can shoot. I give him credit," said Hobey. "I can't stand the guy but he's got an eye for the hoop."

"They only beat us by two. Maybe tomorrow."

"I need a beer," said Hobey.

"Tonight?"

"Why not? Beer never hurt anybody. My old man says so."

"Well, we can't get any, so what?"

"Leave it to your uncle," said Hobey.

He slipped out of the door. The lighting was poor on the motel grounds. He saw Coach Jones at the far end of the row of rooms, entering his own quarters. He ran swiftly past the pool. He looked across the street. There was an all-night tavern, a lone bartender. He made a dash, walked into the place.

The barkeep said, "Hey. You one of them basketballers got your tail beat tonight?"

"No. I'm a salesman for a sporting goods house." He produced identification. He always carried false papers. "Give me a six-pack, please."

"Okay." The barman looked at a pair of customers at the far end of the bar. "You smoke?"

"What you got?"

"Columbia gold, man. You got twenty-five bucks?"

Hobey said, "Let me see it."

The man slid an envelope across the bar. Hobey palmed it, sniffed at it. He put thirty dollars on the bar.

"You'll love it, man." The bartender put a six-pack of beer in the paper sack. "Ain't supposed to sell for takin' out. You mind, now. Go out the side door, there."

Hobey said, "Keep the change," and went through the exit. He looked up and down the street, then raced through shadows back to the room.

Jim said, "Hey, that was quick."

"Wait'll you see what I ran into."

There were cigarette papers in the envelope. The marijuana exuded a pungent aroma. Hobey quickly rolled two joints, handed one to Jim.

"I don't know," Jim said. "Last time we did this there was trouble. Remember?"

"That was a year ago. We did too much. Just take it slow and easy. Sip a little beer. It's mellow, man."

"It does help a guy sleep," said Jim, lighting his reefer. "Just don't get any wild ideas."

"I'm cool," said Hobey. "Got to think of something for the game tomorrow. This helps."

"Got to sleep," said Jim. "Got to be ready."

"We're ready. It's the coach. That Crowell. Everything is for his style."

"Cappy and Ruman are with it. You dig them?"

"So we're better'n they are. We'll show up. We'll be there."

"Sure. We'll be there."

They smoked and sipped. At twelve they turned out the lights and got into bed, still sipping and puffing.

Gus Grumman, delegated by Coach Jones, prowled past the rooms, making certain all lights were out. It was a job he did not fancy. Grumman was a man to keep his knowledge of what went on strictly to himself. When he came to the room occupied by Barker and North he stopped dead in his tracks. There was a crack beneath the door, the air conditioning was running. He leaned low and the unmistakable odor of the weed was wafted to his nose. He checked his list and peered at the room number. He shook his head and ambled on his route.

It was none of his business, he reckoned. There were

many things he knew about those two boys, including the connection between Jackson and Barker. If he were asked, if it came to a showdown—but it never did. He wished Mrs. Harper would come back from Europe. She was the only person in whom he would confide.

Coach Jones was in the room assigned to Dean Botley. Coach Holder was present, as was Mrs. Cross. The atmosphere was uneasy, tense.

Botley said, "It was a well-played game. Two points, my goodness. A very narrow margin. However . . ."

"I benched your boys," said Jones bluntly. "They were lousin' it up. They're not in shape."

"Ahem. You are the coach. It was an auspicious start for the season. It is just that . . . Well, the Barker family and the North family have been generous with donations to Harper School. Now, believe me, I will not—repeat, will not—interfere with your coaching. I do want you to be aware of the situation."

"What situation?" demanded Jones.

"That which I just stated," said Botley stiffly. "I want Harper to progress, to be prosperous so that we can give the best in education."

"You wanted a basketball team that would put Harper on the map," said Jones. "Holder here was doin' a good enough job for a small school needin' funds."

Botley threw up his hands. "I can't deny what you say. Maybe we can do something with those two boys. Maybe a talking-to would help."

Mrs. Cross said, "It will not help. I've talked with them.

They are very polite, nice boys. But they have their own notions."

Jones said, "You've talked to 'em. I've talked to 'em. They got talent; they could be good enough to make the team a winner all the way. With Caponetto playin' like he is and the Crowell kid and Ruman improvin' all the time, we could win the conference. With North and Barker doggin' it, we can't. From what I hear, Battin School can take us nine games out of ten."

"Ah yes. Battin School," said Botley.

"They are definitely the best," said Holder. "They beat us by a dozen points every time we played them."

"We got a great player in Crowell," Jones told them. "The rest of it is in the air."

Mrs. Cross asked, "Isn't there something odd about that boy? He doesn't seem to fit our pattern at Harper."

Botley coughed. "His family also contributed to our fund. I think we can accept him so long as he behaves himself. He has done well in class thus far and he has behaved."

Jones said, "He's a loner. Just leave him to me."

"Well," said Botley. "You're the coach."

The meeting broke up on that note.

Kathy North was in bed but wide awake. She said, "He's really terrific, isn't he?"

Marion Thompson said sleepily, "Right on."

"And Sig Ruman. He's a different man these days."

"You want to double-date with Willy and Sig?"

"Willy doesn't look at anyone but Pam."

"Your friend Pam. Now go to sleep, will you?"

"Pam's okay. In her way. A female jock. An A student. What does he see in her?"

"She minds her own business. Will you go to sleep?"

"There's something mysterious about Willy. He's so polite and pleasant. But he's not with it. Like he's over there some place."

"Wherever he is you'll get there. Sleep!"

"I'd really like to know him, what there is about him."

"You won't learn from me. Will you sleep?"

Marion turned on her side and put a pillow over her ear. Kathy lay on her back staring at the ceiling. Basketballs whirled through her head. They were being juggled by the boy from California.

Sig Ruman was going on as usual. "Coach sure don't take anything from anybody. Setting North down, the captain. Barker, the star. And you're not even bushed after playing the whole game."

"I was raised on the full-court press," Willy said.

"I wasn't. But I'm learning. Never worked so hard. Feels good. Like I'm maybe the five-and-a-half man instead of the sixth man, you know? We couldn't hold those Centrals with the passing game and the stall, I know that. Coach is right. If we had more fast men, if Joe and Hobey would get into shape. Lots of ifs in there. They'll make some kind of trouble. They're wild, those two. 'Specially Hobey. He's always had his way. Money, a car in town, everything."

"Uh-huh."

"Ambs is okay. Cappy's terrific. You don't know how us three have improved this year. Coach is tough but he's all right."

"He's solid."

"The rest of the bench is nothin', pal, nothin'. They just can't run fast enough and far enough."

"They fill in."

"Sure. I couldn't play the whole game at top speed."

"You will."

"You think so? Coach has got me so I don't know if I'm a guard or a forward. He's got me playing man-to-man where I'm needed. Coach . . . well, and you. I appreciate how you've helped."

"Forget it."

Sig was silent for a moment. Then he said, "You notice how Kathy North's got eyes for you?"

"Nuts."

"I was watchin' her from the bench. And when we came on the court second half."

"You better watch the game."

"She stares. When she leads the cheers she keeps taking peeks."

"Sig, you are absolutely something. Now let's get some rest. I'm having breakfast with Brock."

"Brock? The black guy?"

"He ain't black. He's brown. And nice. Regular."

"How come we're having breakfast with him?"

"Not you, pal. Brock and me."

"Huh. That's strange, man. Real strange."

81

"Strange to you. Unstrange to me."

Willy closed his eyes and went to sleep. Sig rambled on, half under his breath, but Willy heard not a word. He had always been able to sleep under any circumstances.

9

AT EIGHT O'CLOCK Willy was dressed, leaving Sig asleep and snoring. He walked out of the motel without seeing anyone from Harper. On the street he saw the tall, lean figure of Brock leaning against a lamppost.

"Hi, man."

"Hi, California. Got a heap around the corner. Take a ride?"

"You're the man."

The car was a neatly kept, four-year-old VW. They coiled themselves within it. Willy asked, "You couldn't get a smaller one?"

"I scarcely got this one," said Brock. "What's your first name?"

"Willy."

"Steve Brock. One of many Brocks. Not really in the ghetto, just on the edge. Papa works for the city. Mama works for the city. It's a black town, Newark. And they like basketball players."

"Lots of places, towns, schools, colleges, they like us."

"For reasons." Brock drove southward. On Broad Street he stopped in front of a cafe. They got out and went inside and a genial black man greeted them. They sat at a porcelain-topped table in the rear, apart from other customers. Brock did not order. The food came on the moment—cereal, fruit. The counterman asked, "You like eggs or pancakes or what? Steve, he eats honky food to keep in shape."

"Eggs and bacon, if you please," said Willy. "Milk?"

"Milk, it is." The man grinned at them. "Weird to see a Harper kid in here, Steve."

"This one's right on."

"Must be if he's with you. He looked good in there last night."

They ate. The eggs were soft and without grease and the bacon was crisp. They each drank a quart of milk.

Brock said, "About Harper College. They take blacks?"

"It they want a basketball team they better had whether they want or not."

"The nigger game."

Willy shook his head. "The playground game."

"Hey, you really do know what goes down. You learn that in California?"

"New York. I spent a bit of time there. And I read a lot about the game."

"Well, it's true. Black kids spend their lives on the playgrounds if they take to the game. We get good by fightin' each other. I'm into getting an education, Willy. Basketball's the yellow brick road."

"Right."

"You know anybody?"

"Not a soul. I'm new here."

"Yeah, but you're going to be a star, man. You're going to turn it upside down. You got style. You got that eye, those hands. Couple of our guys wanted to take you out. You know? Make you foul out, shove you around, any old thing.

Me and some others told 'em no way. Watch and learn, we said. Those other dudes on your team, they're for the birdies."

"First game," Willy told him. "Couple of them will be okay."

Brock was silent for a moment. Then he asked cautiously, "How come you're here, Willy?"

"Long story."

"Your folks out there?"

"One there. One here."

"Oh. Hey, I'm sorry I asked."

"It's all right. They've been divorced for years."

"So you got shifted around."

"You might say so."

"I'm not pushin'," said Brock. "It just seemed like . . ."

Willy interrupted him. "I know. You get a feeling about a fella."

"Right on. You and me, what a combination on the court, huh?"

"Heavy."

"Harper College. A nice little school in Bucks County. Small-time basketball but nice. Clean-cut. No big deal. Graduate and you got alumni looking after you, right?"

"I guess that's part of it."

"They got pre-med. Oh, I looked it up after we bombed them last year. Harper School, I mean. Found out it was prep for the college. I'm ambitious. I want to be somebody. To go to Harper College, that would be a first step."

"Make application."

"You think I didn't? Now I'm waiting. Black is beautiful.

I'm not a chicken. I know I could go to a big city school and maybe make it. And maybe not. But at Harper I'd be a star. Right?"

"Uh-huh." He realized that Brock was not bragging, merely stating a fact. He warmed toward this young man who knew what he wanted, he who had not hitherto been able to communicate with strangers. "Tell you what. I'll have my folks write letters to Harper College. It may not do any good but it's worth a try."

"You'll do that?" Brock's eyes were moist. "Hey, I knew you had to be a good dude to play the way you do."

"What's so good? If I go to Harper I'd sure like to have you on my side."

"Never you mind. I know you're stickin' your neck out."

"No way," said Willy.

"Tell me! Look, if you ever get into anything heavy in this town you call me, hear?"

"Heavy?"

"Lots of bad things comin' down in Newark. It's a wrong city."

"Tell me a city that's not wrong."

"How about California? L.A. and all?"

Willy said, "I never thought much about it. The newspapers, they're full of bad vibes. Like somebody's being murdered every day. Malibu, it's quiet. Plenty law." There was a city and there was the Valley and there was Beverly Hills where no one could take an evening walk without the cops asking questions. He should take more interest, he thought. He should be more aware.

They talked about the two coasts, east and west. Brock

was better informed than Willy. It was interesting to discuss their opposite worlds without argument. When Willy looked at his watch it was almost time for the morning workout.

"Hey, Steve, I got to get outa here. Practice."

"Holy mama, me too," said Steve. He jumped up and went to the counter. Willy was reaching for the check when Brock picked it up. He began to protest, then backed off. He had been asked to breakfast; he divined the pride with which his new friend paid the bill.

Brock drove like a contestant in a demolition derby. Weaving in and out of the Saturday traffic, he did everything but climb over slower vehicles. A siren sounded and a motorcycle cop pulled up alongside, looked in, said, "Hey Steve, you late?"

"Right on."

"Okay." The siren wailed again and they were within a block of the motel in jig time. The policeman waved and yelled, "Beat out their brains, Steve!" as he drove away.

"Civic pride," said Steve dryly. He pulled up in front of the motel.

They were all there, staring. Botley, Mrs. Cross, the coaches, the squad seemed all big eyes. Willy crawled out of the little car and said, "Be checking with you, Steve."

"Hey, here's my phone and all." He had a three-by-five card carefully made out. "See you on the court. I'll be coverin' you like the mornin' dew."

"You should live so long." Willy felt lighthearted, pleased, amused. "Get with it, pal."

Brock drove off, tires screeching. Willy faced the Harper contingent. No one said anything as they filed to the bus and

87

the station wagon. Sig Ruman looked angry. They sat in the back of the bus near the cheerleaders.

The noise level was very low as the bus pulled away. North and Barker were buzzing to the other players. Glances were thrown back at Willy. Everyone had recognized Steve Brock, it seemed. No one was pleased that Willy had been with the star from Central High.

Willy asked, "What is this?"

Sig said angrily, "Consorting with the enemy. Like you're going to throw the game or something."

"You got to be kidding."

Kathy North suddenly leaned forward and spoke distinctly. "Did you have breakfast with him, Willy?"

"Sure. He invited me. He's a terrific guy."

"He plays clean basketball," Kathy said, making her voice heard throughout the bus. "What did he want with you?"

Willy almost said something about Harper College, but restrained himself. "Just to fan. You know, basketball."

"You like him a lot?"

"A whole lot better than some people we know." He was astounded at himself. He had never said anything like that aloud in his life.

Kathy said, "I'd like to meet him if he's that nice."

"Maybe some time when we're in Newark again."

She sat back down. Her cheeks were pink but she held her head high. She caught her brother's gaze and stared him down. She nudged Marion.

Marion said, "I think it's neat, having breakfast with the guy you play against. Real neat."

"Sportsmanship," said Kathy.

88

The other girls took their cue. They chimed in, admiring the clean, clever play of the Central High boys, praising Willy for accepting Brock's invitation. It did not sound right to Willy's newly sensitive ears.

He said, "Hey, there's nothing to it. Can't two guys have breakfast without brewin' up a hurricane? What is this, the Soviet Republic?"

Coach Jones turned in his seat, then crouched in the aisle. "That's enough! I never heard such talk. It makes no difference who Crowell had breakfast with. He showed up on time for the bus. I don't want to hear any more."

There was little more talk until they came to Central High. They filed into the gym and the boys went to the dressing room. Willy watched from the corner of his eye. North and Barker were whispering to the bench players. Caponetto was first to be ready. He came to where Willy and Sig were tying their shoes.

"Barker and North," he said. His dark eyes were bright. "And a couple of the subs. What the hell kind of minds have they got?"

"It's jealousy," said Sig. "They're sore because coach set them down yesterday."

"They keep saying Willy's an oddball. I don't think you're an oddball, Willy. I think this team would be zilch without you."

"They know that," said Sig. "That's what's killin' them."

Willy looked at his two friends. "You know what? Up until now I wouldn't give a hoot to hell. I've been thrown out of more schools than most of you ever saw. Lately, it's been different. Thanks."

"Don't thank us," said Cappy. "You play it cool, man. You go your own way. Best we all should. Backbitin' and gossip, the hell with it."

"Right on," said Sig.

Coach Jones was calling for attention. He was at the blackboard with a piece of chalk. "Now hear me. You did a great job holding them yesterday. If you want to win this one here's the way you do it." He made dashing X's and O's on the board, connected them with curving lines. "You're X. You keep moving in these directions. I mean you don't stop. I'll be using everyone on this squad this afternoon. Maybe only for a minute until the breath comes back—because you're going to run and run and RUN."

He looked at Holder, who nodded and said, "This is new to you fellows. I didn't teach this. But I believe in it—the fast break, the press. Against a team as good as Central it's the only chance we have."

No one spoke. There was a knock at the door. Coach Jones said, "Okay. No big talk, no yellin'. Save your breath for the game. Get goin'."

When they were introduced there was no booing. The applause was faint but it was there, a vastly different reception than that of yesterday.

Willy whispered to Sig, "It's like Brock says, they love good basketball."

"It sure makes you feel better," Sig responded.

The Centrals received the standard ovation, feet stomping, cheers rattling, cheerleaders prancing. Steve Brock winked at Willy, raised a clenched fist. Coach Jones said no more, merely gestured for them to get onto the floor.

90

They went out with the varsity—Ambs, Barker, North, Caponetto, and Crowell. Central played their big five as always—Carter, Jelly, Brown, Washington, and Brock. The referee brought out the ball, the horn sounded, and the game began.

Brock said, "Here you go, California baby."

"Right with you," said Willy.

Brown tapped to Jelly, who passed to Brock coming down. Willy ran step for step. Brock passed to Carter. Cappy was all over the Central forward. They wrestled to a jump ball. Carter towered over Caponetto. Willy watched Carter. The ball came toward Brock.

Willy was there, bending low, stealing. He got the ball and wheeled, looking downcourt. Nobody was there.

He dribbled, circling, swift as an adder, darting in and out. Barker and North finally got downcourt and he passed to North. Jelly covered North, who bounced the ball in the direction of Barker.

Brock stole and took it roaring down to the Central side. Brown was already there. He patted the high pass into the basket and Harper had lost a golden opportunity.

Jones stood up. Ruman and Maloney entered the game. North and Barker sat down. The coach spoke to them in unmistakable terms. Willy was bringing the inbound pass down the boards. Cappy ran a fast circle around his man. Willy gave off and went into the corner. Cappy snapped the ball to him. Brock tried to block but Willy outjumped him and delicately put the ball in the basket to tie the score.

Now all the Harpers ran down. Willy got a hand on it, again knocked it loose, recovered it. Sig was open. He took his shot. The ball went into the net and Harper had two.

North and Barker returned to the court. Their ears were pink, their jaws set. Their eyes, however, were glazed, Willy thought. The Centrals had possession and on they came like five stallions.

North and Barker ran. Under the basket Willy was fouled. He put the ball into play to Cappy, who roared down the line. North and Barker went stride for stride. Cappy, covered, passed to North, who gave the ball to Barker. Willy did a pirouette and was open. Barker fed him the ball, but he threw it twice as hard as necessary.

Willy took it in his big hands and flipped it into the basket as Brock overstepped his position.

Brock said, "Hey, no fair makin' me look bad."

"Did it to yourself," Willy told him, and then was running again.

The Centrals took it down and this time no one could stop Brock from making his move and taking the perfect jump shot.

It went that way. With all the Harpers running, applying the press as best they could, the score mounted to twenty-two for Central, twenty for Harper. Willy had scored fifteen of the Harper points. Again and again he was open and North and Harper had to feed him.

Central took one of their rare time-outs. The cheerleaders came out and Kathy was smiling at Willy as she led them. Willy was listening to Coach Jones.

"All right, you're runnin'. Now watch them change their style. They don't like us being so close. Ruman, Hagen, Rohm, Maloney, you go in while we figure out their strategy. Just press 'em, keep on top of 'em. Feed the ball to Crowell."

The subs doffed their warm-up jackets. The regulars put towels over their shoulders and sat close to Jones and Holder on the bench. Play resumed.

The Centrals came out passing. The ball went around with dazzling speed. They resembled nothing more than the Harlem Globetrotters. Being taller and stronger than the Harper players, they made them look like kids chasing stolen hats in a schoolyard. With the huge Brown in the low post, they got the ball to him and he sky-hooked it through the basket.

Willy brought it down once more. Now Brock switched on him and Brown loomed, arms waving. Willy passed to Barker.

Barker took his shot from fifteen feet out, an easy jump. He missed. Brown blocked Willy and Brock got the rebound.

Back they went to the passing game. They revolved in circles going down the boards. They were technically perfect, with the addition of a few frills, such as between the legs lay-offs just to confuse the Harpers. They scored again with ease.

In a very few minutes they had a lead of eight points. Then Coach Jones sent back the varsity, rested, fresh and with blood in their eyes.

Willy dribbled. Brock was all over him like a tent. Cappy took a low pass. The Centrals went man for man. Cappy shoved one back to Willy and set a pick at twenty feet from the board. Willy jumped and one-handed it neatly. It fell through and the lead was six points.

Now the Centrals went to their passing game. The Harpers flew at them like a pack of bluejays, pecking at their eyes with open palms, trying to destroy their timing, waving arms, flagging the passes. Central muffed one chance, Brown to Brock, and Willy was in there stealing the ball.

Barker ran for the basket, Jelly in pursuit. Willy led with the toss. Barker took it cleanly, leaped—and missed the lay-up. Brown was underneath, towering, palming the ball. Willy backtracked as fast as he could. The long pass was meant for Brock. Willy uncoiled his highest leap of the day.

The ball was in his hands. He saw an opening and dribbled into it. He faked Carter into the seats and shot from fifteen feet, a natural for him. The Harper contingent screamed with glee.

The Centrals returned to their ground game. They were like thoroughbred racehorses coming down the court. Willy ran with Brock but could do nothing to interfere with his consummate skill in ball handling. The pass went to Jelly who scored over Barker.

Still they ran. The Harpers gave it the gamest try possible. Willy scored again from outside. Brock scored when Brown blocked off Willy. Back and forth it went. Once Willy saw Barker open and passed to him. Again Barker missed a comparatively easy shot. The horn ended the period.

In the dressing room all was quiet. They were down six points. Coach Jones ignored the blackboard.

"You can't keep up with them. Barker, North, you sit down for the start of this stanza. Barker, you missed two easy ones. Any reason?"

"They were coming in and I lost my timing."

"Those cats are always comin' in," roared Jones. "You got to expect they are comin' in. They are good. They are better than us. But we fought 'em tight yesterday. Why not today?"

"Yesterday beat us up," muttered North.

"You and Barker. Everybody else in playin' up to his potential. I've warned you."

"You can't bench us," North said. "I'm the captain."

"You *were* the captain. On the court from now on, Willy Crowell is the captain."

"You can't do that. I was elected."

"Not by me," said Coach Jones. "Sue me if you like. I'm runnin' this team and so long as I do, you're not the captain. A captain stays in condition."

"We'll see about that."

"You can look all you want. You can squeal to high heaven. But you and Barker are weak in the knees after five minutes runnin'. Ruman and Maloney may not be up there yet but they're learnin'. You two are learnin' nothing. Now the rest of you get out there and do what you can . . . Press 'em and run 'em."

Willy said, "Just a minute, coach."

"I don't want to hear from you, neither."

"It's just that I'm a new guy. I think Cappy should be acting captain. The guys know him and he's good at holding us together."

Jones scowled. Then he said, "You don't want the job?"

"Cappy can do it better." Willy's voice was very quiet.

Coach Holder said, "Crowell has a point there."

95

"Okay," said Jones. "Okay. Just so you bring that ball back without throwin' it away." He glared at Barker and North. They glared back at him.

It was a bad situation, Willy thought, going back to the court. The team was now hopelessly split. He had been in situations of this kind before. No good had ever come out of them. The subs were improving, that was true, but none was of the caliber of North and Barker at their best.

Still, he understood the problem of the coach. It was unquestionable that North and Barker could not hit top speed for a sustained period of play. He had looked for them in spots where they were needed and found them missing. He had taken a couple of risky shots and luckily had made them. He could not maintain that pace and he was well aware of it.

Brock greeted him. "So now we got you where we want you. Got the big dudes on the bench, huh?"

"Uh-huh."

"They weren't doin' doodley-squat," Brock said. "What's the matter with those two?"

"I wouldn't know. They do not love me."

"I could dig that."

"It's just a game," Willy said. "Take it easy on me this half, will you?"

"I'll drive you through the boards."

"I'll be good," Willy said. "Honest."

With that he ran around Brock and stole the tap from Jelly. He found Sig loose and fed him. He went down and took the right corner. Sig faked to Maloney and gave him a nice, high pass. Willy scored.

Central romped, eager to score again. Maloney, a big,

96

quiet red-haired kid, somehow got in the way of Carter. The ball rolled free and Jelly touched it before it went out of bounds. Cappy took it, feinted for Willy, gave it to Ambs, who held it high, pivoting. Willy went in the back door. Ambs fed him. It was a lay-up.

The Centrals began to put on pressure. They passed the ball around, they drove, they set picks. Somehow the Harpers managed to be in the way of scoring. Ambs deflected a pass and Cappy took it and went down with it and passed to Willy. Brock was on him. Willy faded left, went right and arched the ball into the basket.

"Hey, now," said Brock. "Who's your pal?"

"Nobody." Willy was off and running. He was tireless on the boards. He had run the Malibu sands every day while in California; he never drank nor smoked. Now he was finding that the hitherto-unnoted Maloney was a fine passer and had a good head on his shoulders. Sig was everywhere, tiring a bit but not letting down. The game raced along like the Kentucky Derby. All of a sudden it was 60 to 60 and six seconds to go. Central took a time-out.

At the bench Coach Jones was leaping up and down. Holder was handing out towels with trembling hands. Barker and North sat apart on the bench, alone together. Everyone was jabbering at once.

"Crowell's got thirty-two points, you know that?"

"Maloney, you're a wonder."

"Sig, you're playin' better'n you jabber."

"Ambs, you the BIG man."

"Cappy, what about Cappy?"

Jones said, "They'll have a set play. I don't know what it'll be. Cover every man and watch Brock like hawks, guys. Brock's their cleverest ball handler."

"Not against Crowell," said Cappy. "Willy's handled him good."

"He's still their best all-around player. Watch him."

Time was called. Jelly had it for inbounding. Willy stuck by Brock like a mustard plaster. Jelly passed to Washington. Carter and Brown stepped in front of Willy. The ball went swiftly to Brock. Maloney lunged—and fouled the classy Central guard.

Brock went to the line. He dropped the first one. He did not miss with the second. It was 62 to 60 for the Centrals.

Cappy grabbed the ball and gave to Willy. Again it was tincanning, doubling in his tracks, spinning through the opposition, looking for an open man. He saw Cappy ducking under and wheeling and gave it to him. Cappy faked a shot, then gave it back to Willy.

From twenty feet Willy shot. The ball rolled around the rim. Ambs tipped it in. "No basket," said the referee.

It was a good call. Ambs had touched the iron rim. It was Central's ball and they took it down fast. Brock rolled it in and Carter picked it up. He shot. Willy jumped, blocked it, then stepped accidentally on the line.

The Harper fans were pleading. Kathy and the cheerleaders were on their knees, praying. Botley was leaning so far out of the stands that he fell against Mrs. Cross.

Jones called time-out. There were three seconds left to play. He said, "Long pass to Willy. Take the chance. It's all we got."

98

With those three seconds left on the clock, Jelly inbounded to Brock. Willy went after him tooth and nail. Brock stopped dead and passed to Washington. As Willy made his move, big Brown set a pick. Brock went low and under the hoop. Sig was a half-step too slow.

Brock leaped into a jump shot that was lovely to see. The ball went through the hoop.

The game ended. Willy grasped Brock's hand.

"Man, that was sensational. That was super."

"Your boy was almost there." He showed white teeth. "Some kind of a ball game, brother."

The Harper fans had come down with the cheerleaders, yelling as though the team had won. The Central crowd was howling, "California! California!" It was a good feeling, a better one than Willy had known. He heard the Central coach tell Jones that they had the conference title in their pockets if they could keep up the pace. He heard Jones reply, "I dunno, pal. There's always problems."

"I can see you got 'em. But good luck."

In the dressing room it was quiet. The players were showering, putting on street clothes. Jones made no speech. He walked among them, talking to each in turn. He came to Maloney and said, "You're my starting forward from now on."

Maloney turned red. "Uh . . . thanks, Coach."

Jones went to Ruman. "You keep in shape and you'll be the other forward."

Sig said, "And in plenty trouble, Coach."

"Trouble is my middle name."

Botley came in through the door. He called loudly, "This is a true moral victory. This was the best game ever played by a Harper team."

North and Barker were already dressed. They went out together, speaking to no one. Botley followed them.

Jones said, "So it's his job. If they quit we got no bench. I couldn't let them play, you know. They were lousin' up the gym."

Gus Grumman, waiting to drive the station wagon, started to speak. Then he shrugged and left.

Sig said, "If they do quit we'll have to dig up a couple of stiffs to sit on the bench. Nobody can win a conference with eight men."

"Nobody," Willy agreed. He was thinking of Steve Brock. He went out and got into the bus and sat with Sig in the rear as before. The cheerleaders were already there, singing the school song with such spirit anyone would have thought the Harper team had won the game. Willy was weary, even thought it was not apparent. There was a mental strain, an emotional strain which transcended physical response to such a contest. It was a game to play and replay in his mind.

Kathy North came and knelt beside him. "You're absolutely terrific out there."

"Your brother won't like it if you spread that around."

"My brother is sometimes a jerk," she said. "My brother wouldn't be so bad if it wasn't for the company he keeps."

"I wouldn't know anything about that."

She said, "Why are you always alone on campus?"

"Am I?"

100

"Well, you and Pam, I've seen you together. Pam's not into boys, you know. Tennis, that's our Pam."

"She's your friend, isn't she?"

"Of course. She's our chairlady. Pam's a great person. But not for parties. I'll be running a small get-together soon. Will you come?"

"Why . . . sure. I guess so. You know, if I'm not busy." He was neither confused nor flattered. He had been a star for a few years. He was accustomed to girls and their little ways. "Let me know about it when it comes down."

He leaned back. She went back to the girls.

10

SUNDAY WAS SUNNY and the air was cool. The tennis court was composition, cupped, the tapes soiled. Pam and Willy came to it at noon.

"You're sure you're not tired after two such tough games?" she asked.

"Not too tired to give you a lesson."

"Willy, how you do talk. I've never heard you so loquacious."

He looked at his newly strung racquet, opened a can of balls, enjoying the sound of the airtight can as it popped. "It's funny, Pam. Between Sig and that fella I told you about, Steve Brock . . . I don't know. Maybe I've been wrong, keeping quiet."

"Living within yourself. Me too."

"You spoke up to Botley."

"A lot of good it did me." She indicated the court. "Harper School doesn't spend money until it must."

"He promised you. He did give the girls more time. Even bought costumes for the cheerleaders, took them on the bus."

"Small things."

"I don't know. It's all new to me. Participating. Trying not to get mad at North and Barker."

"You'll get angry," she said. "Sooner or later. They are goof-offs, those two." She paused, then added, "But you sure made a hit with sister Kathy."

"Oh?"

"Oh, yes indeed. My best friends told me about it."

He said, "She seems a nice enough kid."

"Kathy's a very nice piranha."

"Wow! I never heard you say anything like that."

"Maybe it's catching."

She walked onto the court. She seemed to change as she bounced a ball at the service line. She stood taller, her features altered, grew harder. Her long fingers wrapped around the handle of the racquet. They began to rally.

Her shots were crisp and deep. He met them in perfect form—he had been raised on tennis courts. The two young people were a picture of grace in action. Very few practice shots went awry.

She peered at him across the net. "Are you ready?"

"Serve 'em up." He had played against top women in the West. They had offered no real competition. He relaxed, standing on the base line to receive.

She bounced the ball, stared at him, threw it up high, came over on a perfect sliced service. The ball went deep to his backhand. He was caught flat-footed. He made a stab at it, set up a short lob. She came in and put it away with a slamming overhead.

He said, "Hey, there."

"You're not playin' with kids, you know," she said dryly.

He took the ad court, laying back three feet. Again the deep service, slanting wildly. This time he drove it cross-court. She was there, anticipating. She sliced it to the sideline. "Thirty, love," someone said on the spectator's bench.

Pam said, "Hi, Kathy. Why don't you climb up there and referee?"

Kathy North said, "This should be good." She was wearing shorts and a tight sweater, white as snow. She had good legs climbing to the high seat. "Take him, Pam."

Pam took the first game. Willy was, he found, a bit rusty. He stretched his arms and they changed courts for his serve. As they passed, he said, "Too good, huh?"

"Good enough." She did not smile. Tennis was her business.

Willy went to the line, center. He bounced the ball three times, building rhythm. He tossed it up and came through. It danced to Pam's backhand. She returned but not deep. Willy was in at the net. He put it away.

"Fifteen, Crowell," said Kathy in high-pitched imitation of tournament umpires.

Willy moved over. He did not try for an ace. He fed forehand and Pam came back with a fine, deep shot. He followed through and felt his game returning to normal. They rallied for eight shots. On the ninth Willy found the ball waist-high and aimed for the corner. He got it and Pam was left flat-footed.

He won the game at love. Kathy said, "This could go on forever. You guys are really!"

They didn't appear to hear her. They went back at it. Pam had Willy at forty love when he suddenly began to apply terrific topspin to each shot. The ball bounced high. Pam made errors. Willy persisted and she began to move back, return

105

each shot. Then he switched to underspin. He won her service. As they passed in changing courts she said, "How come you took up basketball?"

"Just one of those things."

"You could be a tournament tennis player."

"Not in the top twenty," he told her. "Not good enough for me."

She nodded. She went deep into her concentration. She served a perfect game. Willy was missing by only inches but she was forcing him. She was, he knew, the best woman player he had ever met. Kathy called the set well, breaking in to applaud good shots but accurate in her judgment.

Two figures strolled onto the adjoining court when the score was five to three for Willy with Pam serving. It was a moment or two before Willy recognized them as North and Barker. He bent, weaving, ready to receive. A ball came rolling onto the court just as Pam started to go into her smooth service.

"Please," said North.

Willy straightened. "Hey, guys. Do you mind? Pam needs a workout."

"The courts are open to all students," said Barker in a nasty-smooth voice.

Willy said, "Supposing the girls threw basketballs while we were working out?"

"Coach wouldn't like it." Barker was enjoying himself.

Willy said, "Okay. Knock it off. There are two courts beyond the fence. Go and play on one of them."

"Like who's going to make us?"

Willy looked over at Pam. She shook her head. He stood a

106

moment in thought. He had been shrugging off situations like this for several years. Nothing mattered that much, he had felt. He walked to the beat of his own drum. It was his way, the way he slid through life.

He looked at the mocking face of Barker, then at North. He said, "Now you know and I know what's goin' down. Two of you, I start a fight, you cripple me. Right?"

"Fight? Who wants to fight?"

"You do. Or else you wouldn't interrupt the school's star tennis player during a workout," said Willy.

Barker said to North, "Seems like California found his tongue. I wonder what else he found besides a nigger pal in Newark."

Willy dropped his racquet. He walked deliberately toward Barker.

A small figure rushed between them. Kathy North said in a loud voice, "You two amscray. Flee the scene. Get lost. I heard all that jazz. You want trouble, I'll see that you get trouble. You dig?"

Joe North said, "You keep out of this, sis."

"Between Pam and me, we'll have you thrown out of school altogether," Kathy told them. "Now, git!"

They looked at one another. Willy still loomed but he had a half-grin on his face. Pam leaned on her racquet and laughed aloud.

"Tough guys," she called. "You tell 'em, Kathy."

There was a moment of indecision. Then Barker said, "Hiding behind a woman's skirts, huh? Always knew there was something creepy about you, Crowell. Get you later."

"When my back is turned?"

107

For a moment it seemed that Barker was about to charge past Kathy. Then North took his arm and led him toward the far courts. They passed Gus Grumman on the way. The old Marine shook his head and went about sweeping leaves from the premises.

Pam and Willy went back to their game. Kathy did not climb back onto the umpire's stand. The spirit had gone out of the exercise. Willy closed it out with little enthusiasm, taking Pam's service forty to thirty. The three sat on the bench in a row, Willy in the middle.

Pam said, "That was neat, Kathy. You did good."

"They'd have given Willy a hard time."

Pam said, "Maybe. Have you ever seen me swing a racquet in anger?"

Willy said, "I believe she could, at that."

"You see? Women are on the go," said Kathy blithely, "How does it feel to be backed up by us?"

"I haven't had a fight since I was twelve," said Willy. "I probably need backing up."

"I doubt that." Kathy looked worried. "You know, Jim was a nice kid until he started to room with Hobey Barker. He was elected captain because they like him. *Liked* him?"

"Maybe Barker's a nice kid, spoiled rotten," said Pam.

"That I doubt," Kathy said. "Ask me about him when he gets you alone. Casanova in person."

"Oh, I didn't know."

"You still don't know. And you never will," said Kathy.

Willy said hastily, "I'm for a shower."

They walked toward the dormitories. The girls talked

108

about women's rights, the committee which Pam chaired. Willy reflected upon several matters: How wonderful Pam looked on the court, what a tough player she was, how cool she behaved. He stole looks at her and her child's face was sometimes clownlike, sometimes brooding, sometimes bright with laughter.

Kathy was different. Prettier, yes. More outgoing, more aggressive. She was as open as Pam was reserved. She seemed to be holding nothing back, prattling yet making sense, a really great girl, a whole lot like the Western girls he had known.

Maybe too much like them? He had never been known as a real swinger with the female sex. He had taken his experiences as they came without losing a pulse beat. It was a bit of a shock to him that he was thinking at all about Kathy and Pam, listening to them talk, walking with them across the campus.

At the entry to the girls' dorm a breathless Marion came running to them. "Hey, you guys. What went on at the tennis court just now?"

"Lordy me," said Kathy. "You mean someone was listening?"

"Mrs. Cross was behind the baize backdrop. As usual, nosing around. She said there was a near fight. She said Willy was always in some kind of a scrape."

"Mrs. Buttinsky," said Kathy. "It was nothing, really. Just my brother and his roomie acting up."

"Mrs. Cross said it was Willy's fault."

"Mrs. Cross is partial to Jim and Hobey," said Kathy.

" 'Specially Hobey. She likes rich people."

"Well, the cat has escaped the bag," said Kathy. "It'll be all over school in an hour."

"I told her I didn't believe Willy would be into anything like a fight," said Marion.

"Thank you . . . I think," Willy said. He started to leave, waving, smiling at them. Pam moved to catch up.

She said, "I'm sorry I caused all this."

"Look, I saw those two hit a couple shots. They're not tennis players. They're pure hackers," Willy told her. "It wouldn't make any difference where it happened. It was going to happen, that's all."

"Still, if you hadn't worked out . . . Thanks a lot for that. If I could play some with you the women would look easy."

"We'll work out," he said. "You're terrific, you know."

"Yes. I know. But all that women's rights talk . . . Not in tennis, friend. Not in tennis."

"Since the game was perfected," he said. "You know the history. Men have . . . advantages."

"They're built different." She flushed her hand, going to her breast. "More reach. More strength. But no smarter."

"You want to know something? I enjoy watching women's tennis. The strategy is clearer, more . . . I don't know . . . Better."

"More like a chess game?"

"That's it."

She said, "Thanks again." She hesitated, then added, "Willy, you're an odd cat. I like you. Stay that way." She turned and ran back to the other girls.

He had thought Kathy was the more outgoing. In the last

110

couple of days he had learned a few things. Maybe he was paying closer attention, he thought. When he wrote his father about Steve Brock he must remember to thank him for sending him away to Harper.

Sig was reading the Newark Sunday *Star-Ledger*. He put it down and asked, "Well, you want to tell me about it?"

"You know already?"

"It's a small school full of gossips, remember? What went down?"

"I'm not sure." Ordinarily he would not have spoken about it. Now he needed an outside opinion. He told Sig what had happened.

Sig said, "Those guys never hit the courts. They went out there looking for trouble. They are really burned." He picked up the newspapers. "The sports page is full of what we almost did to Central. Brock's the hero but they really get it up for you. Man, you're a hero! And they step on Hobey and Jim. 'Coach Jones showed fine judgment when he yanked the former star players for Harper who were dogging it.' You see? But these guys blame it on you."

Willy said, "That's plain dumb."

"They never won prizes as students. They think they know, therefore they can't learn. So long as they were on top around here everything was a laugh. Barker got away with murder. I think Mrs. Cross covered for him a lot. Jim, he just tags along. Barker drinks more beer than water, you know."

"How should I know?"

"It's an open secret," said Sig. "Botley may or may not be

111

onto them. I think Holder suspects, but he's Mr. Nice. He never makes waves."

"Mrs. Cross. I keep hearing things about her."

"Botley's left hand. His spy. Probably she's more loyal to Hobey than to Botley. I didn't want to tell you these things, Willy. I know I got a big mouth. I try not to retail dirt, though. I figured you'd find out sooner or later. Those two cats are bad news."

"And without the bad guys we haven't got a basketball team."

"That's about it."

"Coach will be blamed. It's always that way."

"Coach showed his guts when he benched them. They'll be after his hide and yours and mine."

Willy said, "My mother always says forewarned is forearmed. I don't know about that. This is a tough go-around."

"If you win, the school loses. If you lose, the school loses. Coach is shaping the team around you. Botley wants that conference title so bad he can taste it. Best we should keep our cool."

"I like it here," Willy said frankly. "I know I haven't said much but you've been a hell of a roomie."

"And you've made me a better basketballer. You and the coach. He couldn't have done it alone. Playing with you, listening to you, believing you. That's big, man, big."

"Coach is okay. The rest of the guys are okay." He paused, sighed. "You're right. Do our thing and keep cool."

Sig, relieved, said, "There. I said it. I've been thinking it and I finally said it."

"Thanks again." There should have been more but he

could not find words. "I have to shower. See you."

"Huh? Oh, yeah. We'll have dinner, right?"

"Sure. Got to hit the books. Don't you?"

"Yeah. Right on."

He went into the shower. He was a bit confused. He felt as if another world had opened with the meeting of Steve Brock, the tennis with Pam, the confrontation, the short talks with the girls, Kathy's obvious interest in him, then Sig's outburst. It had all come so quickly that he was not prepared.

All these people of whom he was thinking had families. Maybe that was a difference, maybe that was something he had never really got into before. He simply did not know about family. Since he'd never had one, he had not missed the absence. He had not really cared about much excepting the basketball action, the surfing, casual acquaintances who had amused him, beguiled him for short periods.

"Heavy," he muttered to himself. "Real heavy."

II

HOBEY BARKER sipped on a beer. "That was a nothing."

"He wouldn't fight. He's not the type," said Jim North.

They were in their room. The afternoon was young, the sun was shining, they were oblivious. They were smarting from defeat.

"He's chicken, all right."

"My own sister," said Jim.

"Girls. Expect nothing from girls. 'Specially nice girls."

"I don't know any other kind."

"Ha! Well, maybe it got him uptight. We've got to get him off base or something. That damn Jones can't ever understand. Crowell is weird. He don't belong in Harper."

"How did your bets come out?"

"How do you think? I took Central and gave ten points. Jackson went along. He's madder'n a hornet."

Jim said, "You know what? We ought to start training."

"Are you crazy or something?"

"Hey, we're good. We can make this team a winner."

"Who cares?"

"Maybe it would be better if we showed up Crowell and Jones by doing our thing."

"Look, Jim. Life is what you want it to be, if you've got

guts. Fun. Games with fun. You want to be a dumb jock like Crowell?"

"You saw the papers. It ain't exactly nothing to get written up like that. And the way they wrote about us. My family, I just hope they never see that write-up."

"My people would laugh. They'd know I was doing my own thing."

For several minutes neither one spoke, thinking of his family. They were restless; they were not happy. Barker was talking big, Jim thought, but the worms were eating at him. They had been the kings of the campus; now they were the jokers. It was as simple as that.

Hobey got up, crushed his beer can, deposited it in the ever-ready paper sack. "I'm going to see Mrs. Cross."

"That old biddy."

"She's okay." He did not confide too much in Jim North these days. He was becoming suspicious of the world around him since things had gone wrong on the basketball court. He pretended to scorn the importance of the game. It had taken disaster to bring home the fact that it was a huge part of him—the stardom, the actual playing, the respect of his teammates.

When he entered the administration offices they were deserted except for Gus Grumman, who swished a mop over the hall floor. Hobey did not call to him but went directly to the office of the dean.

Mrs. Cross sat behind Botley's desk. She was a widow, childless, a woman who did not take the students to her heart. Only Hobey seemed to have real access to her.

116

He said, "Hey, you look good sitting there. Too bad you don't have the job."

"Dean of Women, that's all I ask. Not more money, just a title. They refuse it to me. They say there aren't enough girls in the school."

"You'll get it. My folks are going to talk with Mrs. Harper when she returns," he told her.

"I'm counting on that." She had a piece of paper before her. She said, "That California boy. You were curious about him."

"Well, you know. He's kind of strange, isn't he?"

She said, "Definitely. And I think I know why."

"Honest?" He pretended indifference. "Something in his background?"

"His father, Hobart, is Rex Ball."

"The big Western star? The new John Wayne?"

"Precisely."

"Then he's entered under a phony name?"

"No. His father's real name is William Crowell. Rex Ball is his movie name."

"Oh, I see."

"His mother is Karen Brevoort, wife of Bosley Brevoort. It is her third marriage. Rex Ball lives in California. Karen Brevoort lives in New York where she still pursues her career on the stage."

"So his parents are divorced."

"When they separated there was a tremendous scandal. I won't go into details but both their names were dragged through the courts and the newspapers. Willy Crowell was in a military school. He was expelled. He was expelled from three private schools before coming here."

"He was thrown out of three schools?"

"For various reasons. Once, I learned, for smoking marijuana. Once having to do with a girl."

"Wow! You mean Willy was a wild, bad kid?"

"He was. You can see that Willy's background was dreadful."

Hobey thought it over. "So that's the big secret about Crowell. Does the dean know this?"

"Of course. It's all in his file."

She had sneaked a look in the private files of Botley, he knew. "Then . . . I don't get it. What's wrong with Crowell being here in school?"

"You mention it to a few people," she said. "Maybe you'll be surprised. I do not believe that his kind is wanted here."

"You mean that I start a little rumor? Get the kids guessing about him?"

"That is up to you, Hobart. But I think we understand each other."

"Well, I don't know. He's the big hero right now."

"Since the dean condones his presence, we must be cautious. I will wait until Mrs. Harper returns and then I will take steps."

"I'll think about it. By the way, did you bet on the games?"

"No." Sometimes her smile was cruel. "In the records it stated he was one of the best basketball players on the West Coast. And all those points . . . No, I didn't bet."

"You're a smart lady," said Hobey. Her nose seemed to

118

come to a sharp point, her eyes were close to each side of it. Margaret Hamilton in *The Wizard of Oz,* he thought with a slight shiver. "I'll be in touch."

He went out of the building. The air was fresher than indoors, yet there had been a large window open behind the dean's desk. He prided himself on being above petty scruples. He had been taught that any means to an end was the only philosophy. Yet he felt uncomfortable.

Gus Grumman leaned on his mop and looked at the retreating back of the youth. Then he shook his head and went back to his chores.

There was a beautiful sunset glimmering through the tall trees, as it had since colonial days. Willy and Sig walked toward the commissary bemused, entranced. Willy said, "It's so different from the West Coast. It's purely grand here at twilight."

"It's so pretty I could sock somebody in the nose," said Sig, who was no poet.

A figure loomed between them and the trees. They stopped and smiled at Coach Jones. He said, "Okay, what went on at the tennis courts today?"

They were taken aback by his abruptness. Willy said, "Nothing important, Coach."

"I heard different. You almost had a fight with North and Barker."

"There wasn't any fight."

"If there's anything I won't stand for it's fightin' among the players. You get that?"

Willy said, "There wasn't any fight."

"Furthermore, I don't want you on those lousy courts. You could easy turn an ankle. You stay off them, Crowell."

Willy said slowly, "I guess you're right. They are uneven and tricky."

"Playin' tennis with girls is not for my guys," Jones went on. "You stick to basketball. You do fine on the court."

"A court is a court," Willy said. "Tennis is a great game, Coach. Pam Stern needs work. I might help her."

"Let somebody else help her. Anyway, she's good enough to beat anyone in her league. Better."

"The great thing about tennis is that no one was ever perfect at it," Willy said. "Nobody, not ever. You can always sharpen your strokes."

"Okay. So let her sharpen them. But not on you."

Willy was silent for just a moment. Then he said, "Coach, for six days a week you're the boss. But Sunday is my day."

"Are you gonna be like Barker and North? Are you gonna give me trouble?" The big man was near to pleading.

Willy said, "You're the best coach I ever had. I'll never give you trouble six days every week."

Jones stared at him. Then he turned on his heel and walked away.

Sig said, "There's a man really has got troubles."

"Plenty."

"You're right. He's a terrific coach. What good will it do him if the team don't win?"

"No good at all."

They resumed their way to dinner. Pam Stern came from the girls' dorm and joined them. "Coach Jones after you?"

"How did you know?"

120

"The whole school's talking. Did he tell you not to work out with me?"

"He sort of hinted."

"He told me to stay away from you."

"He did what?"

"Oh, on the court, the tennis court."

"Remember, we talked about Morristown. Is there a good court there?"

"Excellent. The club gave me a season pass. I can use it any time."

Willy said, "Next Sunday we'll get a ride in."

"Against the coach's orders? I can't let you do that."

Willy said, "There was a time when I'd have told the coach where he could go and what he could do. Now I'm passively active, if I know what I'm talking about. Which maybe I don't, but I do know I've been in trouble just about all my life and there's nothing can be done about it."

Sig said, "Hey, you got a right. I mean, Sunday is our day off, the only one all during season. Next week it's Battin and they are really rough. Maybe the next weekend we're off—I think we play Friday at home. Amboy Academy, the Dukes. Then it's a grind."

They entered the dining hall and got in line with trays. Kathy North came to join them. There was no training table but the players had orders as to diet. Pam selected salad and chicken and rice. Kathy ate roast beef, potatoes, gravy, tomatoes, and a big piece of pie a la mode. The others regarded her with no envy. Their habits were formed by the sports they had always enjoyed.

They sat down and Kathy said, "My brother is furious at

121

all the talk going around. Hobey doesn't care. He never cares about anything that I can see. The coach jumped all over Jim late this afternoon."

"A lot of fuss over something that didn't happen," said Sig. "That's the trouble here. Everything is blown up all out of proportion."

"Small school and some small minds," said Pam. "But it's better than most."

"You can say that again," Willy agreed. "I should know."

Kathy looked sharply at him. "Is it true that you attended at least three prep schools in the West?"

"Uh-huh."

"So there's another story going around," said Kathy. "Mysterious Willy Crowell."

"Any more?"

"Yes," she said and stopped.

Now the story of his past was out.

"I see," said Willy. His food suddenly tasted flat. It was hard to swallow. He kept his face calm.

"Look, I'm having a party after the Battin games," said Kathy. "Will all of you come?"

Pam said, "Gee, I'm sorry, Kathy. But I know your late parties. I'm working out Sunday morning."

"With me," said Willy. "But, hey, thanks a heap."

Sig said, "All right if I come alone?"

"Certainly." Kathy said no more. She was disappointed but determined. She ate her dinner and left them, smiling.

Pam said, "I'm afraid we hurt her feelings. She loves giving those parties and having everybody she likes around her."

"She's got me," said Sig. "I'm a nice kid."

"You're not Willy. Kathy has the big eyes for Willy."

"I wish you birds would lay off," Willy said. "Her brother would kill her if she went out with me. Also, I don't have time for girls. Excepting Pam."

"Oh, boy," she said. "Now that will get around. Willy Crowell plays tennis with Pam because . . ." She broke off.

Sig said, "Yeah. They'll be cutting your initials in the trees. W loves P. It'll be real cute."

"It'll be just another hunk of trouble," she said. "Maybe you ought to go to the party and skip the tennis, Willy."

"I've been to parties that got me in trouble. I never got into trouble on the tennis courts." He finished his meal. "You two. Don't worry about me. Almost nothing can happen that hasn't happened to me before."

He left them. He had to be alone. He could see it all coming to a head now. He could hear his father yelling, his mother weeping. He had tried to play it cool, to be laid back and easy. He liked Harper, he liked Jones despite his attitudes, he liked Sig a lot. And Pam . . . He was amazed at how much he liked the cool, graceful tall girl.

He had never felt this way about a girl before. The experience was warm and good but a little scary. He knew he would defy the coach, the dean, the campus talk to be with her. The workouts were a convenience. It was her relaxed, easy company that soothed him, made him feel more secure than he had ever been in any relationship. He walked toward the trees. The sun had gone down and there was an unearthly light from its afterglow. He walked into it, his mind going around like a squirrel in a cage.

12

ON MONDAY WILLY was early at practice. The girls were finishing a new, complicated dance routine, weaving the pompons, kicking, pirouetting. When he paused Kathy came running, flushed, beaming.

"You like it?"

"Cool," he said. "Inspirational."

"Battin always has a show biz bunch of girls. We're trying to top them."

"Great."

"I'm glad you like it." She flashed him her best smile and left with the other girls.

He went into the dressing room. Coaches Jones and Holder were sitting on a bench. He greeted them.

Jones said, "Knew you'd be the first one. I want to talk to you."

"Okay." He began to change clothing.

"Holder's going to take over for awhile. I want you to watch."

"Watch?"

"You'll get your workout. It's just that I'm makin' some changes."

"I see."

"Holder tells me Battin has got a long bench. Eight or

nine top players. We got to match 'em."

"Uh-huh?"

"We got to work our bench all week. I mean work 'em."

"That's okay by me."

"And we got to get North and Barker into shape."

"Uh-huh."

"We are going to work that pair. They will run. I mean they will RUN."

Willy said carefully, "Does that mean something about me?"

"It means you're the playmaker. I'll be talking to you while they run. They're not going to like it. After the Central games I formed opinions. I mean to follow my notions."

"Yes, sir."

"It's going to cause trouble, right?"

"I'd say so."

"Are you game?"

"What do you mean?"

"Will you stick, no matter how the wind blows?"

Willy said, "Why shouldn't I?"

"That's all I need to know."

Sig came in and then the others. Jones went into his office. Holder looked at Willy, half-smiling.

"It's going to be rough," he said, "You'll be under pressure."

"What can I do? He's the boss."

"Oh, you can handle it on the floor. It's the reaction off the court that will be strong. The North family and the Barker family are strong supporters of Harper."

Willy shrugged. "So I've heard."

126

"On the other hand your parents have contributed."

"You mean money makes the school go?"

"Botley seems to think along that line. On the other hand, he hired Jones. You see?"

"Uh-huh." It was a time to be noncommittal.

North and Barker came into the dressing room. They went to their lockers without greeting Willy and talked together as they changed clothing. Willy took a basketball and went out into the gym. He took the first shot from midcourt, missed, came in for the rebound and made a long one. He retrieved under the basket and did a backward lay-up. The muscles tightened by the weekend of basketball and tennis loosened up.

Kathy North said, "Hey, great!"

She was sitting on a chair at the far end of the gym. He looked at her and shook his head. "You better take a powder."

"I'm going to. I'll be having another party soon. Will you come?"

"According to the schedule."

"Must you always be with the team or with Pam?"

"It sort of works that way. Pam needs practice."

Kathy said, "Like a hole in the head she does. All right, Willy, if you're going to be like that."

"I'm sorry. I'd love to go to a party. Maybe it'll come around that way."

"Don't hold your breath." She was gone.

He went back to work. The week was starting out like others he had known. He had been in so much trouble in so many places that he could smell it before it enveloped him.

The siren whistle of Jones brought everyone to attention. The entire squad was now in the gym. They gathered in a group.

Jones said, "I'm sticking by my decisions. We're starting a new lineup. Maloney and Ruman are in. Barker and North are sixth and seventh men. Any questions?"

"I'm no sub," Barker snapped.

"Take it up with whoever," Jones told him. "North?"

The former captain hesitated. He did not look at Barker. "You're the coach."

"You finally understand that? Get yourself in condition and you'll play."

North said, "I . . . Okay, whatever."

Barker said, "Ruman is not in my class and you know it."

"Ruman's in shape. You're not. Get this: I want the conference title. The only way we can get it is to run the opposition to the pits. That's my game; that's the way we go."

Barker said, "And feed our California star? Sure, your boy, your pet."

Jones waited a long moment. Then he said, "Barker, there's no doubt about it. You either stay and shut up—or you go. Make up your mind."

Barker started to walk toward the door. Then he turned and stood in the rear of the group. His face was fiery red, his neck muscles bulged. He said thickly, "I'll stay."

Jones did not glance his way. "This is now a ten-man team. Maybe it hasn't got all the skills we need. But it's got legs. Whenever I see one of you anywhere at any time I want to see you either walking real fast or jogging or run-

128

ning. Legs. LEGS." The thin boy dumped a bag of basket-balls which rolled around the floor. Jones called, "Take one and dribble. Run and dribble. Stay low and keep moving until I tell you to stop."

Willy worked up and down the right lane. It was good thinking on the part of Jones, he knew. Ball handling plus running would sharpen reactions, reflexes, strengthen the body as well as the legs. However, it would work only as well as it was practiced. Barker and North were needed. He knew that, Jones knew it. They had the real basketball know-how. It would be a struggle of wills between them and Jones from now on.

The whistle startled him with its shrill command. Jones said, "All right. Split up. Five against five. Man on man. The press. We're working on the press."

Holder paired them off. Willy drew Fred Hagen, who had been first string the previous year, a fair guard who had not learned the new system. He let Hagen come to him, put on the moves slower than usual, giving Hagen every chance to follow and learn. In fifteen minutes Willy was still fresh and Hagen was puffing.

Willy said, "Take it easy. Bend your body at the hips. Keep your arms wide and loose."

Hagen said wearily, "I . . . don't . . . know . . . if . . . I can make it."

"You'll make it," Willy told him. "Just keep at it."

"That's . . . easy . . . for you . . . to say." But Hagen grinned and when the whistle shrilled again he had his second wind.

129

Willy bounced the ball. He saw North and Barker side by side on a bench. Their heads were in their hands. Jones was standing before them.

The coach said, "There's something wrong with you two. Why are you behind the others? Why are you in such bad shape?"

They had neither breath nor desire to reply.

Jones said quietly, "You're both basically good players. You should be the backbone of this team. I'm not going to tell you more than I have already. And I'm not playin' favorites—not now, not any time. Get that in your heads. You show me you can do it and you'll be starters again."

Willy went out of hearing. It was a situation in which he hated to be involved, even as an innocent bystander. The practice session went on until the entire squad was near to utter exhaustion.

Jones said, "Same time tomorrow, same drill."

In the showers Ruman said to Willy, "You think we'll all be alive when Battin comes in Friday?"

Willy shrugged. He had no answers. Jones was betting on his notions. The rest was up to the squad.

North and Barker were walking across the campus, limping, stiff-legged. North said, "You think we can get in shape? I mean really?"

"We'll do it. We got to send down Jones and Crowell."

"Is that why you didn't quit?"

"You know it, soldier. What's more, I'm for a reefer and a beer."

"You got to be kidding."

130

"I'm out to prove it can be done. Beer and pot in moderation won't hurt anybody. The pros use 'em. Didn't you ever read those exposé stories?"

"You believe them?"

"Where you at, Jim? With the rest of the turkeys?"

In their room Jim brought out the beer. Hobey uncovered the cache of marijuana and rolled a reefer. They settled down, legs outstretched. They inhaled as the cigarette went back and forth between them.

"My legs sure hurt," said Hobey.

"Jones says run. We run."

"Like the dumb middle-age joggers. Don't tell me their legs don't hurt."

"Who cares?" Jim sighed. "What about the weekend? We'll have time off."

"Jackson knows a couple of chicks in Morristown. When I place the bets I'll set it up. We'll do New York. In spades."

"Hey, maybe we could get to see the play that Crowell's mother is in. That'd be a kick."

Hobey said, "Right on. I know a guy can get tickets for any show on Broadway. Jackson put me onto him."

Jim asked, "You sure about this guy Jackson? I mean if it was ever known we were bettin' against the team . . ."

"Forget it. I own Jackson."

"What about the point spread?"

"I give Battin at least five. No more, on account of those write-ups Crowell got for the Central games."

Jim asked, "Why not take five and bet on us?"

"Because I figure Battin can beat us by six or more."

"I see. Still . . . It's risky."

Hobey said, "Have a puff and relax. Everything will come up roses."

It was an hour before the Battin School game on Friday afternoon. Willy Crowell was dressed for action but he was alone in his room. The final out of the album "Joyful Jazz" by pianist Father Tom Vaughn was flowing from the stereo. There was a knock on the door.

When he opened it Gus Grumman entered, cocked an ear and said, "Classical jazz. Got onto it in Paris after the war. Is that Father Tom?"

"Yes."

"You know him?"

"He was rector of the church in California. Still is."

"Episcopalian. He's one of the best in the world. You know that?"

"I know."

"Been a crummy week, hasn't it?"

"Uh-huh."

Gus gestured. "Silly little girls out there waitin' to get you to sign their silly little books, huh? All that stuff about your famous pa and ma."

"Uh-huh."

"Some folks actin' crazy."

"Uh-huh."

"I'll get you out the service entrance downstairs."

"Thanks."

"They're waitin' for you at the gym. Some think you won't show up. All that stuff in the Morristown paper."

"I know."

"You don't wanta talk about it. No way you should talk about it. I been around before I come here, y' know. I like it here. Do you like it here?"

"I did."

"You ashamed of your ma and pa?"

"No."

"Just people, ain't they?"

"That's the way I see it."

"You ain't scared?"

"I don't like it. I hoped it would . . . go away when I came here."

"It'll never go away."

"Uh-huh."

"The coaches are scared it'll affect your game."

"I know."

"You been practicin' bad all week."

"Uh-huh."

"Fella gets his head screwed up, he don't concentrate good."

"Uh-huh."

"Okay. Lemme count your friends." He held up a hand. "Ruman, your roomie. Pam Stern. The coaches. Caponetto. Maybe a couple others. And me."

"Thanks."

"I been watchin' you. I watch a lot of people. I just wanted to tell you to go out there and give 'em what for."

Willy listened to the thundering finish of the "Battle Hymn of the Republic," turned off the set. He faced Gus

133

and said, "You know, I was playing that tune to get myself up. It has . . . power."

"My grandpa fought in that war, the Civil War."

"You just did me a big favor," said Willy. "Let's duck out of here and get to the game."

13

IT HAD INDEED BEEN a weird week. They had come at him from all directions. Botley had tried to talk to him, to apologize, to offer sympathy. The dean had not sounded sincere. Willy's sensitivity to people had warned him that his stay at Harper would be altered, that it could not be the same. Not that anyone seemed to care about the scandals of the past, it was just that they changed. He was notorious. It had driven him back into the shell from which he had been beginning to emerge. Through no fault of his own, he had been shoved into unwelcome public view.

He entered the dressing room as Jones was turning from the blackboard. He recognized the inbounds play outlined thereon. The coach looked at him, started to speak, refrained. Someone in a falsetto voice asked, "Giving out autographs, Crowell?"

Jones wheeled around. "Enough of that. One more word and someone's goin' to get thrown outa here for good!"

"Sorry I'm late, Coach," said Willy.

"You know the plays. We worked on 'em all week. Battin is the team to beat in the Conference. That's all. Get out there, team." He stopped Willy with a gentle hand. "You all right, kid?"

"I'm all right."

"Let's see what they got, huh?"

"Yes, sir."

"Stopped talkin' again, have you?"

"What's the use?"

"Maybe you're right. Just so you play your game."

They went onto the court. Battin had brought a bus load of fans. They were noisy but disciplined. The Harper girls were waving the pompons and exhorting the student body. A ricky-tick little band made as much music as was in them, which was not classical jazz. Willy heard only the few cries of "There he is. Rex Ball's son. Isn't he cute?" He steeled himself against it. He had been foolish to hope that it would not follow him east. He should have known better. His entire experience had taught him that people love nothing better than gossip about the famed.

Now he was at the bench, removing his warm-up clothes and the Battins were being introduced. They were a brawny lot, not as tall and overpowering as the Central High players—but they had the bearing of champions. He sought out his man for the afternoon, Bobby Hartner, an All-State forward. Hartner was a blond boy exactly Willy's size and build, long-armed, with huge hands. He looked formidable.

The little band stopped. The home team was being introduced. Willy's name was called. He trotted out to shake hands all around.

From the Battin fans a united shout went up, high and shrill, "Hollywoooood! The kid from Hollywooooood . . . Boo-ooo."

The Battin cheerleaders leaped to their feet, waving their arms in anger, shaking their heads. They tried to start a cheer, "Crowell, Crowell, rah, rah, rah!" It drew feeble response. The Battin people had read the newspapers. They had a mark and they meant to shoot at it. Willy felt himself flushing.

Kathy and her girls were on the job. They led a yell, "Battin, Battin, Battin, yeah, yeah, yeah!"

There was some handclapping. Then a voice from the opposing stands yelled, "How's your ma, how's your pa?"

Caponetto growled, "Lemme get that guy," and started for the stands. Willy grabbed him and held on.

The Battin coach stood up. He shouted, "No! No!"

Bobby Hartner came to Willy. He stuck out a hand and said, "Every school's got 'em. Stinkin' muckers. Good luck, Crowell."

"Thanks," said Willy. "I'll need it."

The horn sounded, the ball went up. Battin had Diamond at center, Fortney and Hartner at forward, Grange and Abelson at guard. They were into instant action.

Diamond outjumped Ambs. Hartner had the ball. Willy followed him down. Hartner bounced to Fortney, Battin's top scorer. Caponetto guarded him with high hands. Hartner faked, went in the back door and scored on a perfect pass.

Pam Stern could not sit in the stands. She stood at the aisle leading to the dressing room and tied her strong hands into knots. Gus Grumman came and spoke in her ear.

"He ain't on his game. He shoulda blocked that pass."

"I know," she responded. She looked at Grumman. He winked at her and nodded.

"Yeah. I know his friends."

"You know a lot, don't you?"

"Yes. Maybe too much sometimes."

She said, "I'm glad you're on our side."

"I dunno about that, either. I do know you can't expect too much outa him this afternoon."

They turned strict attention upon the game. They saw Ambs get the downcourt high post, saw him feed the ball to Willy. They saw Hartner, all arms and elbows, crowding in. They saw Willy unable to get loose. The ball went to Jim North, who scored to tie it up. Harper cheered.

Grumman said, "He shoulda been loose under the basket."

"Hartner's a terrific player."

"Willy's better. If he's on his game."

The action was hot and heavy. Battin exercised a figure eight that should not have worked. It did, and again Hartner scored. There was a foul on Ambs and Hartner made the two free throws and it was six to two.

There was no doubt of the skill of the Battin team, Pam thought. They put in substitutes as the period went on and each seemed as proficient as the first-team men. Coach Jones sent in Barker. For a few minutes the Harper team seemed to pick up speed. Willy scored twice but Battin returned with three field goals and another foul. North and Barker went out. Nothing seemed to work for Harper.

At the end of the half the Battin team had a ten-point lead. Harper's squad filed off, grim-faced. Pam reached out on impulse and touched Willy's arm.

She said, "On the ball, pal. Offense. Offense!"

He stared a moment, far away, then jerked his mind back to the present. He managed to grin. He said, "Hey, thanks."

In the dressing room Coach Jones said, "They're good but

138

nowhere near as good as Central. Crowell, you're not playing up. Hartner's no Brock. What's wrong?"

"Just can't handle him, I guess." Willy was thinking of what Pam had said. He had not been playing offense, he had been defensive. It was in his head, he knew. He had been lacking in concentration on the precise problem of playing against a team like Battin.

Jones said, "You can play Hartner. But I'd rather have you play the basket. I want everyone to feed Crowell. You guys understand? Ten points. I want them back."

There was more but Willy scarcely heard. He was thinking about his mother and father. They must have learned about the fuss by now. He knew his mother read the Morristown paper. He wondered if they cared. He wondered if they knew how it affected him to have the "Hollywooooood" label attached to him. It was just another matter he had never discussed with them.

It was not truly what others thought of him. It was what it did inside him, in the core where he dwelt, the way he felt about himself and his place in the world. The half time ended.

Pam awaited him. She did not speak; she looked at him and he knew her friendship, her worry, her real concern for him. He ran onto the court.

Ambs outdid himself on the tip-off. Hartner went for the ball and Willy beat him to it, then laid off to Caponetto. The Harpers flew downcourt. Hartner clung like a burr. The pass went to Ruman, who was guarded by Grange. Sig faked, then gave the ball to Cappy.

Hartner stuck like glue. Willy leaned left, head-faked.

139

Caponetto gave him the low pass. Willy swiveled and went into the jump shot over Hartner's head. He scored and the difference became eight points in favor of Battin. Barker came in for Maloney.

Battin brought it down. Hartner stayed close to Willy, then darted for center court. He took the pass from Grange, gave to Abelson, who sent it around the horn as Harper guarded well on every man. Diamond went into the low post and there was muscling under the basket but no foul called.

Cappy made a stab to steal from Grange. He missed and went off balance. Willy came in to back him up.

The ball rolled loose. Sig was on the spot, gave it to Willy, who passed downcourt to Cappy. Barker ran into the lane and Cappy gave him the ball. Barker shot—and missed. Battin roared down to score.

Harper called time-out from the bench. Jones was stone-faced. He said, "Maloney, go in there."

Barker sat down. Caponetto took the ball from Ruman and trotted along the center path. Willy went into the right lane. Hartner stuck to him. Ruman swiveled into position. The ball went to him and he whirled, held it high.

Willy leaped within five feet of the hoop. He took the perfect throw. He dropped it into the net.

The Harper fans went wild. Eight points now, with time running and Harper playing heads up ball. Battin came back with their merry-go-round, stalling a bit but looking for a shot. Harper was on them, every man working close. Hartner took a pass near the center line, looked for help. Willy stole the ball from him, clean as a whistle. Hartner seemed dazed. Willy passed deep to Ruman, who dropped

140

in two points. The margin became six.

Battin took a time-out. Willy went to the bench. He was in time to hear Jones say, "North, Barker. You see how this game is played?"

North was silent. Hobey Barker said, "I see you're playing your favorites."

Jones fixed him with a glare. "Barker, go to the showers."

"You can't . . ." Barker choked. He grabbed a towel, threw it around his head and departed.

Jones asked in low, cool voice, "Anyone else feel I'm playing favorites?"

No one spoke. Jones said, "You're runnin' and you're playin' the game. Keep doing just that."

Battin had regrouped, Willy saw at once. There was a skinny black boy named Hanson in the place of Fortney at forward. Hartner looked as though he could kill. Battin went into a full-court press. They were splendidly conditioned and they had played together for two or three seasons. They were good, very good. They blocked a shot from Ruman and Diamond got the rebound and away they went.

Willy was down as quickly as Hartner. They shadow-boxed, cleanly and legitimately for position. Willy got inside, but the play went to Hanson and the lean lad made a terrific long shot. Again there were eight points between the two teams, with the champions back in form.

It was nip and tuck and more of it for several minutes. Willy scored three times. Battin scored again. Now only four points separated them. The clock was running down. Willy moved in on Hartner. He was playing the ball and the game now, not the man. He got a hand on the ball.

Sig was guarding his man close by. He seized the ball. Willy was already going for the Battin basket. He took Sig's toss and scored. It was now forty-two for Battin, forty for Harper, with a few moments on the clock.

They were roaring in the old Harper gym. Kathy and the cheerleaders were dancing at the far end. Pam clasped her hands together. Gus Grumman's shoulder touched her as both leaned forward.

Battin had the ball. They courageously took it down, disdaining the stall. Fortney reached for a pass from Hartner. Willy took a chance, throwing himself through the air.

It was a clean interception. He dribbled down the left lane. He saw Hartner coming, stopped dead, let Hartner overrun him. He passed to Sig, who went to Cappy. Willy was in the corner. Cappy's pass was accurate. Willy took his jump shot over Hartner. He scored.

For the first time in the game it was tied. Battin took a time-out. At the Harper bench Jones was standing tall and proud. He said, "Maloney, take a breather. North, you're in. Get that ball."

North was fresh, rested. He guarded the throw-in. He rattled Crowell. Willy was lightning-swift getting into the pattern once more. He laid the ball to Sig, who was open and set. Sig carefully made his shot. Harper led by two.

Pam whispered, "Let them hold on. Let them hold!"

"Let 'em charge," said Grumman. "Let Willy work."

The Battin team retained its poise. They brought the ball down with care, passing only when a man was open. Willy stayed with Hartner. Sig stayed with the big, high-score man, Fortney. Time was running out. It was a low-scoring game, mainly because of the fine, fast footwork of the Harpers. Battin was looking for an open man to score the tying basket before the clock could end the game.

Willy moved, watching Hartner. He knew they wanted to get the ball to their star who might set up Fortney. When his instinct propelled him, he moved around his man. The pass was indeed to Hartner. Willy slapped it. Cappy, always on the play, snapped up the ball. Sig was already running. Cappy threw a long one. Sig ran under it, caught it over his shoulder. He ran under the basket for a lay-up—and missed. A groan went up from the Harper fans.

Battin would not now be denied. They raced down and Fortney counted for two. Once more the game was all even at forty-four.

Battin flew into an all-court press. Cappy inbounded on the bounce to Willy. He stole a quick glance at the timer. There were three seconds left. He dribbled right, then left. Hartner crowded him. He spun, bounced off to the nearest man. It was North. He set sail.

North came with what speed he had left. He crossed over, his man following. He stopped, ducked. Willy was under the basket. Ambs set a pick on Hartner. North flung the ball.

It was a poor pass. It was too high and off the mark. Willy left the floor as if propelled by dynamite. When his hand closed on the ball he was already shooting.

Ten men crouched, watching. The leather rolled around the hoop. Slowly, gently it dropped into the strings. The horn ended the game. Harper had defeated the reigning champions.

Pam stood up very straight. "He did it."

Grumman said, "He charged."

Then they were enveloped and separated by the throng

143

which came down to cover the court like a pack of ants. The team had to fight its way through the cheering student body to get to the dressing room.

Hobey Barker's locker was open. It was also empty. For a moment every eye was upon it, then all was forgotten as the Harper squad tasted the joy of victory.

The celebration was still going on when Jim North entered the room he shared with Hobey Barker. The air was redolent of beer and grass. Hobey sat deep in a chair, watching television. He looked up and said, "Well, you almost blew it. That was a lousy pass you gave Crowell."

Jim sat down. "You think I did that on purpose?"

"Your money was gone anyway, huh? The point spread."

"I wouldn't have done it."

"You what?"

"I almost blew it, that's right. But I wasn't thinking of the bets. I was tired. My legs hurt. I just made a bad pass, that's all."

"Hey, what's that mean? You chickening out on me?"

Jim drew a deep breath. "I'm broke. I can't go to New York with you tomorrow night."

"Come on, I can loan you the dough."

"No loans. I've got to write home for enough to pay off. My folks don't think too much of that."

"Hey, man, have a puff and a beer and you'll feel better."

"No."

"No? What gives with you?"

"Hobey, we've been friends. It's been fun. But you quit and I kept running this week, and coach played me and I did some good—and we beat Battin."

144

"Big deal. Wait'll tomorrow. It'll be even money and we'll clean up when they win."

Jim shook his head. "No bet."

Hobey arose and towered over him. "You mean you're backing out on everything?"

"I'll move out of here tomorrow if that's the way you want it."

"Why you . . ." Hobey gulped. "Now wait. Let's talk this over, pal."

"Look, I'm still your friend. But I saw something this afternoon. I saw Crowell pull the game out. Everything was against him but he pulled it out. I can't go against him nor the team. I can't do it."

"I see." Hobey reached for a sweater. "Okay. I'll call Jackson and call off your date. I'm going to New York tomorrow night, believe me."

"And you're off the team."

"I'm off the team, the school, the whole bit."

"What's that mean?"

"It means the hell with everything. I'll transfer out of here as soon as my folks can arrange it. I may not even finish this term. That's what it means."

He stalked from the room. Jim sat back and wiped his brow. The television yapped at him. It was not good company. He felt alone, deserted. He had the sudden wish to talk with someone. He had been so exclusively close to Hobey for the past three years that there was no one to whom he could turn. He went to his desk, uncovered his portable typewriter and began a melancholy letter to his folks back home.

14

COACH JONES was in the room occupied by Willy and Sig. He asked, "What are we going to do for a tenth man?"

Sig answered, "There's a little bitty kid named Peale. He couldn't make the squad last year. Saw him in the stands yelling his head off."

"How small is he?"

"He could walk under a snake," said Sig. "But he's got the guts of a bear. And, Coach, he can run."

"He can run?"

"Like a scared rabbit."

"I'll talk to him." He went to the door, paused. "You guys believe in my idea of hard work, strong legs?"

They nodded. They grinned at him.

Jones said, "We'll get through the season."

He left them. They sat with their feet outstretched. They were weary and happy and worried all at the same time.

"Like we always said, we need Barker and North. We haven't got Barker," said Sig.

"North stuck in there."

"That last pass was a bummer."

"He was under pressure."

"Weren't we all?"

"His sidekick had walked out on him."

"Okay. I'll admit he ran this week. He's in better shape than he was."

"He's a good sixth man."

Sig beamed. "How about that? North is sixth man. Cappy is captain. I'm a starter."

"That's the way the mop flops." He uncoiled, stretched, and went to the door. "Think I'll take a walk."

"A walk? You outa your mind?"

"Stretches the tired muscles."

"Now mine! I'm stretchin' out on the bed."

"Sleep tight."

Willy went out into the cool September night. He walked toward the lake. He knew in his heart she would be there.

She was walking slowly, as though waiting for someone. He came up beside her and took her arm and gently squeezed it. "Hey, there."

She said, "Hi."

"Nice night for a walk."

"Not for you."

"There's a bench near the water."

"Really? I never noticed."

It was the bench somewhat protected from casual view, sometimes occupied by furtive pairs of boys and girls. They found it empty and sat down, not too close together, each struggling with native shyness.

She said, "It was a game and a half."

"It was good."

"What about Hobey Barker?"

"He cleaned his locker."

"You need him."

148

"Yes. You know a boy named Peale?"

"Petey Peale? He's a tiny tiger."

"He's our man, it seems."

"He's a midget but he's rough and tough."

"We'll take him."

There was a frog on a lily pad croaking away, seemingly happy. The air was still and a moon was flirting with a bank of clouds. They sat silent for a moment or two.

He said, "You were hangin' in there this afternoon."

"It was a tight squeeze."

"No practice today?"

"I went out early and hit on the bang board."

"Not good enough." Then he said, "Hey, you hit a lot. How about taking off Saturday night for the Knicks game in New York?"

"Basketball?"

"I dig the pros. I learn from watching."

She said, "All the way to New York for that?"

"Well, if you're not into it . . ."

She said hastily, "It's just that you took me by surprise. How'll we get there?"

"We're off after the game. Grumman will drive us in. Take the bus from Morristown, grab a bite, we're there."

"Sounds like an adventure."

"I've reserved the tickets." He stopped, flushing in the dark, hoping she wouldn't notice that he was abashed.

She touched his hand. "I'm glad."

"Uh . . . glad?"

"You think I don't know what you've been going through this week since Mrs. Cross blew the whistle?"

"Mrs. Cross?"

"Who else? She's a female rat. She and Hobey are like that. Ask Gus Grumman."

"Why should she do that to me?"

"Hobey Barker."

"That's hard to believe."

"I don't say he put her up to it. She's always looking for a rich kid to lean on. Hobey's it."

Willy said, "You don't know how I wish none of it had got into the papers."

"Or around the school. Those itsy-bitsy girls hanging around." She chuckled. "Maybe you like that part of it?"

"I'd rather be dead. Hey, thanks for the—uh—sympathy. Old Grumman, he counted off my pals. He put you in there."

"We're a campus item, didn't you know?"

"You're kiddin'."

"You don't walk with other girls. You don't play Kathy's game. You hit tennis balls with me. It's a small world here."

He said, "A campus item, is it?"

"Well . . . you know. Gossip."

He slid an arm behind her on the back of the bench. He moved closer. "Does it upset you any?"

She said, "It's never happened to me before."

"So you don't know?"

"I don't know." She was flustered.

"If it's an item—that's all right with me."

She turned toward him. The move was so abrupt that they bumped noses. He slid his hand up behind her head. The moon struck across them. They looked at each other. Then their lips came together.

150

It was a brief kiss. They were not ready for more. He hugged her and she nestled against him for a moment, then pulled away and stood up.

"I'm chilly. Should we go in?"

"If you say so."

They strolled back toward the campus. Deep in the brush at river's edge Mrs. Cross poked out her head, made a face at their backs and scuddled toward the administration building. In the dark she ran into the waiting figure of a man.

She screeched, "Oh-oh-oh!"

Gus Grumman said, " 'Scuse me. You takin' a nice walk?"

"You . . . you scared me to death. What are you doing out here?"

"Mindin' my own business," said he. "Good night, Mrs. Cross."

She went on. He watched her, shaking his head. Tomorrow night, he promised himself, when he took in the kids. Tomorrow night in Morristown he would send his message abroad.

On Saturday afternoon Petey Peale was in a uniform which had been hastily fitted to his undersized frame. He was a red-haired kid with a wide mouth and piercing green eyes. He said nothing in the pregame excitement, but his jaw was set hard and his eyes followed every move made by the coaches.

Jones introduced him as the new member of the squad and said, "What's more, since he knows you players from last year he may get in. Battin's comin' at you this afternoon. Just keep moving with or without the ball and we'll see what happens."

They went onto the court. The stands were full and the noise was terrific. Kathy and the girls outdid themselves. The little band played defiant martial music.

Battin played defiant, almost perfect basketball. Willy's thirty points was the most ever counted against them by an individual, but they kept coming back and coming back with Hartner and Fortney. The final score was Battin 68, Harper 62.

As they were about to take their showers in an atmosphere quite different from that of the previous day, Coach Jones said, "Peale, you did good. We need a bench. When Barker quit, it hurt. You can all see that. Little as he contributed, a team needs every smidgen of help it can get. Be on hand Monday and we'll see what we can do to mend the hole with the little guy. He looks like a good little guy to me."

They applauded and Petey Peale went deep red down to his naked waist as he ran for the cooling shower. It was a wise move by the coach, Willy thought, to welcome the new boy in such terms. However, they were missing a star who was a foot taller than his successor, a kid who couldn't make last year's team. A good ploy but it solved no problems.

15

THE NIGHT WAS DARK, the moon had gone, a drizzle dampened the Firebird which sat in Jackson's garage. Hobey Barker said, "You're pretty happy for a dude who's been losing up until today."

"Gamblers don't cry," said Jackson. He took the check Hobey had written and put it in a drawer.

"Where's my date?"

"She'll be here. You in a hurry?"

There was something wrong with Jackson's attitude. Hobey asked, "Are you sore at me? I couldn't stop Crowell from scoring."

"You couldn't and you can't. You're off the team."

"Hey, I never shaved points, no matter what the bet," said Hobey angrily. "I just gave you the lowdown."

"Fine lowdown you gave me. I ain't mad at nobody. I'll handle any bets you wanta make from now on. Don't get yourself in an uproar."

A girl walked into the garage. She was wearing a dark dress slit up to mid-thigh, high-heeled slippers, and a transparent raincoat. She had blonde hair swept down across her forehead. She said, "Some night to go to New Yawk."

Jackson said, "Hazel Brown . . . Hobey Barker."

"Pleased to meetcha. Where we goin'?"

Hobey said, "Dinner, a disco, whatever." He did not find Miss Brown very attractive. She had a pug nose and wore too much makeup.

"You got an ID to make the disco scene?"

"I've got everything needed.

Jackson said, "He's hip, Hazel, you dig?"

"You told me that already. Let's go. Rain. I hate rain. You drive careful, you hear, Hobey!" She had good teeth when she smiled.

Hobey said, "I'll be in touch, Jackson."

They got into the car. She chattered all the way along the Thruway and into New York. He scarcely listened. Jackson's impolite demeanor had upset him. The windshield wipers played a scratchy mournful tune until he parked in an underground cellar and escorted Hazel up into the early evening of the city. The lights reflected on the slickness of the uneven sidewalks as they hurried to the Mexican restaurant he had found on East 34th Street. At the bar he was first forced to produce his fake identification. Hers was authentic, he presumed. They had a marguerita apiece. They were escorted to a table and still she rattled on, telling of her job as a manicurist, of the men she had known, of the hundred details of her daily life in which he was completely disinterested. He drank another marguerita but felt no cheerier.

There were two movie houses on the street and she chose one showing a new-style Alfred Hitchcock which was dreary and unworthy of the master. The tequila did not further his inner well-being. He was not accustomed to strong liquor. He wished for beer and marijuana and peace and quiet. He

154

wished for his mother and father and the comfort of home.

It had all gone wrong. It had begun the moment he met the California kid. He had known then that it would not be as it had in the previous time at Harper. Now Jim had defected, which left him alone in more ways than he liked to consider. And there also was something wrong with Jackson, with his masterful relationship to the garage man gambler. And he was not happy with this date that had been arranged for a gala evening. He mooned through the movie.

It was still raining when they came out of the theatre and found a cruising taxicab. They headed uptown to a disco Hobey knew.

They passed the Ascot Theatre where Karen Brevoort was appearing in *The Windsor Affair*. It occurred to Hobey that he had planned to see Crowell's mother in the play. He could not imagine taking Hazel to a Broadway show.

At the door of the disco the doorman said, "Hiya, Mr. Hobart. Got a neat lady again, I see."

They went inside and Hazel giggled, "Mr. Hobart. That's a good one. Like Jackson, he's 'Mr. John' when he's talkin' to those people."

"What people?"

"Oh, you know." She was suddenly evasive.

"You mean the bookies?"

"Bookies? Huh, not Jackson. He's . . ." She stopped.

"I see." It burst upon him like a bomb. Jackson was not laying off the bets. Jackson himself was booking them. He was taking Hobey's money for himself, making certain of a profit, no matter who won the games. He swallowed hard, realizing his inability to do anything about it.

155

He shrank from the enormous din that was disco music, a sound he had always loved. They checked their rain garments and Hazel rushed immediately to the floor where dozens of females dressed as she was gyrated and wiggled. Hobey followed, thoroughly without enthusiasm.

Pam and Willy took a taxi on Eighth Avenue and went uptown. The game had been close and exciting and very swift, with few fouls or time-outs. Willy looked at his watch.

"We can still make the theatre in time," he said. "Okay?"

"Of course. I'm excited, really excited."

The rain was still falling. Traffic was slow as molasses in February. He fidgeted and she noticed because he was usually so calm, so within himself. She said nothing, aware of the cause of anxiety. His uneasiness transferred itself to her. She knew the fear of the unknown.

The taxi finally struggled cross-town and stopped before the Ascot Theatre. The marquee lights blazoned the name above the title of the play, "Karen Brevoort." Willy paid the driver and they got out of the cab in their raincoats, hatless, scurrying to the alley leading to the side door.

They were just in time. Willy's mother came swiftly, holding an umbrella over her head, stately, tall in the light of a single bulb. He blocked her way.

"Mother."

"Willy! What in the world . . ." Her large, lovely eyes went to Pam. "What a tall girl! So nice for you."

"This is Pam Stern."

"Pam . . . Stern . . . The tennis player?" She held out a hand. "I follow the game. Once was Hollywood champion. A Hollywood girl beat you in the Nationals. Yes. So nice."

156

He said, "Mother, about that letter. You know, the one asking you to help get Brock into Harper College."

Her manner altered slightly. "Darling, what do I know about Harper College excepting that your father went there? I mean, it's his job to handle that problem, isn't it?"

"Problem? Mother, Brock's a first-class student, basketball player, and a fine guy."

"Is he? Do you know that?"

"I know it." He took a deep breath. "Mother, it isn't because he's black? I mean that didn't stop you?"

"Now, Willy, you know I have no prejudices. My goodness, Pam here is Jewish, isn't she?"

Pam said, "Half-Jewish. Proud of it, Mrs. Brevoort."

"Of course. The Jews are a great race. And the blacks . . . theatre is full of them, welcomes them. Really. It's just that . . . I don't know this Brock, do I?"

"I could bring him over. You could meet him."

"Oh, I'm far too busy . . ." A deep automobile horn sounded three blasts. "That is Bosley. I must run, children." She leaned to present her cheek for Willy's kiss. "So good to meet you, Pam. Best of luck for the tournaments. I'll be watching the TV. Good night, darlings."

She was gone. Pam took Willy's arm. He was trembling. She held tight. They walked to the mouth of the alley and saw the big black limousine working its way through the traffic. Mrs. Brevoort did not look back.

Willy said dully, "You see? I wanted you to see."

"I saw."

"You dig?"

"I dig."

"Should we walk to the bus?"

"Yes." She held tightly to him all the way. They arrived in Morristown without more than small, impersonal dialogue. To their surprise Grumman was waiting. They got into the station wagon.

Grumman said, "Spent the evening in town. Had things to do. Guess there's no use waitin' for Barker. He's got his own car and driver. That fella Jackson, the garage guy and bookie."

"Bookie?"

"Every town has its bookie. You oughta know that."

"I know enough to stay miles away from them."

"Yeah."

"Sure glad you're here, the rain and all," said Pam.

"Just so you kids beat the curfew. Not that Botley's all that strict. Few minutes, he don't want to hear about it. Mrs. Cross now, that's a horse from a different stable."

"She seems to get around," said Willy.

"That she does." Grumman grinned. "More she gets around, the more I get around. She don't like me much."

They came to the school and Grumman went to park the wagon. At the girls' dorm the boy and girl lingered. The rain had softened. They stood under a dripping small tree.

She said, "I'm sorry about your mother. I'm truly sorry."

"I'm used to it. I never had a family. Never even had anybody I . . . I cared to have."

"Thank you for trusting me, Willy."

"It's more'n that. Girls . . . you're more'n a girl."

"Well . . . I guess I dig that, too."

"Shoot, when I try to explain I goof it up. You see . . .

158

The way it's been . . . Nobody ever wanted me.

"Oh, no!"

"Oh, yes. Father and mother separated. She married, didn't want a kid around. He lived with girls, couldn't want me in the setup. So they sent me to schools."

"Alone. With no one behind you, backstopping."

"That's it. Yeah . . . backstopping. I reckon I needed that. I mean figuring everything out on my own, it didn't work. More I tried, the worse it got. I didn't fall in for what everyone else was doing. Oh, sure, I did at first. Then trouble. Then I didn't know from Dixie. Then they sent me here."

"You were getting a handle on it here."

"Was I? Well . . . lots of that was you. I didn't realize it at first. Now I know."

"Willy. We're just kids, they tell us."

"Seventeen. Maybe that was kids once. Maybe for different people it's kids now. Not for you and me."

"Because we've been around? Maybe, Willy. Maybe."

"Mother and father have been around. And they still think 'Jews' and 'niggers.' You think that doesn't make me feel grown-up?"

"My mother is Irish through and through. She's a great person. My father is a Jewish storekeeper. They sacrificed to pay for my tennis. I made enough to help them last year and I'll make a lot more. They come first."

"You the only kid?"

"Just like you."

"Your folks do everything for you. Mine offer me money. I've got enough money from grandma and that's lucky. I keep telling myself I don't need them."

"Everybody needs."

"I thought I didn't."

"But now?"

"I know that I do. Sig, Cappy . . . Brock . . . the coaches, the team." He took a deep breath and looked through the fading drizzle to the tall trees. "Here. Maybe . . . yeah, sure . . . Harper—Harper College." He choked a minute, then got the words out clearly and strongly. "And you."

She said too quickly, "I'm your friend."

"Oh." He turned away, looked at the trees. "Sure . . . Okay."

"Willy."

"Uh-huh."

"I feel . . . young right now. Too young."

"Is there some dude on the tennis tour?"

"No, Willy, no. This is all . . . new to me."

"This all? This all what?"

"The way I feel. It's been tennis and study. Now it's the way I feel about you. That makes me feel young and scared."

"Oh." He laughed deep inside him. "Good."

He drew her close. They kissed. She relaxed for a brief moment, her lips soft. Then she ran away into the dormitory. He walked to his room on air.

Grumman was watching Mrs. Cross, who was clad in a cloak, watching Pam and Willy. He looked at his watch. Curfew had struck a half minute prior to the separation of the couple. He made a note. Then he went on his rounds. He was almost satisfied with himself.

160

An hour later he heard a car drive up at the perimeter of the campus. He waited, anticipating the event. He saw Hobey Barker, not quite steady, making his way to the window, partially concealed by the ivy and shrubbery. He saw Jim North open the window. He moved into the open and called, "Barker. Just a minute there."

Barker faced him. "All right. You got me. You been laying for me."

Grumman looked up at Jim North. "You might's well hear this. Barker's wrong. It's my job to patrol. Layin' for him wasn't necessary."

"All right. Report me. Late for curfew."

Grumman said, "How about the booze?"

"Prove it." He was sullen.

"Don't wanta. Booze is bad enough. How about the pot?"

"Now you just wait a minute . . ."

"You want me to call the cops and have your room searched?"

"You . . . you wouldn't do that." Fear had now intruded.

"You think not?"

"My folks . . ."

"Your folks have been too doggone good to you, Barker. That's part of your trouble. You're lucky you got me around."

"Lucky? Some kind of luck."

"You heard me. Because I'm gonna tell you something. I'm gonna tell you the team needs you. Maybe just for a few plays now and then. But it needs you."

"No way I'm going to eat dirt."

"Yes, you are, Barker. You're goin' to quit the beer and the grass and you're goin' to try and get in shape. And you're

161

goin' to apologize to the coach and the team. And you're gonna ride the bench while that gutsy little Petey Peale plays. And you're goin' to do it startin' right now."

"You can't tell me . . ."

Grumman said, "I'm tellin' you. It's that or the dean. And the dean means expulsion and whatever your folks want to do about it."

Jim North said, "Hobey, please. It's what I've been trying to get over to you."

"It's blackmail. I'll . . . I'll . . ."

Grumman said, "You'll go inside and think about it. And I'll turn you in for curfew, which'll keep you on campus for a while anyway. But I won't mention the other stuff unless you keep at it. It's a deal I'm makin' you."

Barker shook his head as if trying to dispel the realization of what had happened to him. Finally, he mumbled, "You got me over a barrel."

"Now you're talkin'. Good night, boys." Grumman walked away. The rain had almost stopped. Barker stood in it, staring after Grumman, then staring up at Jim North.

16

THE BROWN GRASS went down the toilet. The beer followed; the cans were stowed in the brown bag, then into the trash can. Jim and Hobey walked in sunshine that Monday. Jim was smiling. Hobey was grim, sweating. They went directly to the office of Coach Jones.

He eyed them. "So?"

Hobey gulped and said, "I want to apologize."

"Not enough."

"I want to work out, get in shape."

Jim North said, "He's serious, Coach."

Jones squared his shoulders. "You know you'll be the eleventh man? That it'll take time to get in condition? That you'll be on probation?"

Hobey said, "I know."

Jones relaxed. "Glad to have you aboard, Barker. Get dressed . . . and run."

"I want to apologize to the team, too."

"They're in the locker room. It's all yours."

"Thank you, Coach."

He watched them leave. North had already proved that he was contrite and ready to try again. Barker? He wondered. He could not put his finger on it but there was something

163

wrong with that boy. However, if he did get in shape to play . . .

He went to the door and yelled, "Peale!"

The little fellow was in uniform. He looked worried. "Yes, sir. I saw Barker going into the . . ."

Jones interrupted. "I've watched you work. For now you're my man. Barker's got a long way to go."

"Yes, sir." Relief was apparent upon the face of Petey Peale.

"Now mind you, if we need him and he's ready, he'll be in there. A lot of ifs, but best to get it on the line."

"Coach, if it's for the team, what can I say? I'm so doggone glad to be back."

"Go and run," said Jones.

These were the decisions which grew gray hair.

Mrs. Cross stamped her foot. Dean Botley sat straight in his chair behind the desk and said severely, "My dear lady, you are going too far."

"Hobart confined to campus. And nothing done about the carryings-on of the Stern girl and Crowell."

"I accept Grumman's reports."

"You believe him before you believe me?"

"In certain circumstances, Mrs. Cross, I must say he seems less prejudiced."

"Prejudiced? You call me prejudiced?"

"In favor of Barker. Yes. I do indeed."

"Remember what the Barker family has done for this school. And the North family. Mrs. Harper will hear about this."

164

"I am going to have enough trouble over hiring Coach Jones, so far as Mrs. Harper is concerned. We need the basketball title in order to justify that and other expenses."

"Those cheerleader girls. You're pampering them. That Stern girl. Really!"

"Mrs. Cross, believe me that I am doing the best I can for Harper School. That is my job. It is my ambition to bring about a balancing of the budget and Title IX. If Mrs. Harper does not agree, I shall resign."

"And I shall be here to see that happen!" She whirled on her flat heels and left the office.

Botley wheeled around and looked out at the campus. He had cut a few corners, he admitted to himself. He had played politics with families who had donated funds. He had gone over his head in hiring Coach Jones. But he had not, he thought, descended to the level of Mrs. Cross.

He hoped it would all come together in the end, whenever that was.

On the tennis court Marion and Kathy were facing Pam. It was damp underfoot and all were taking it easy but Pam was missing shots she would ordinarily have put away. She finally shook her head in despair and said, "Not my day, kids."

They sat on the bench under a late September sun. Kathy asked, "You have a good time with Willy in New York?"

"Wonderful."

Marion said, "But something's wrong."

"Not a thing. Really."

Kathy said, "Something's wrong with Hobey. Jim says he's going back to the team."

"That's wrong?"

"It's not Hobey Barker."

"Maybe he got the smarts all of a sudden," said Marion.

"Not Hobey. He's confined to quarters, which may have something to do with it. Otherwise he's up to something."

"You believe that?" asked Pam. "You mean something to do with Willy?"

"I've known that cat for three years. Kathy's his friend's sister. What he does is all for Mister Barker."

Kathy said, "Oh, I don't know. He's a spoiled brat, and all that. But Jim seems to believe he's got himself straightened out."

"Jim told you that?"

"This very morning."

Pam asked, "What's with those two anyway? I mean, why aren't they in condition to play basketball?"

Kathy and Marion looked at one another. "You haven't guessed?"

"Haven't thought much about it."

Kathy said, "Beer and grass."

Pam said, "Oh. I see."

"You're not shocked, amazed?"

Pam said, "I was on the tennis tour, remember?"

"You mean those dudes go in for stuff like that?"

"The best of them tried it and quit. The rest—some do and some don't. Those that make it big, they don't, believe me. I'm surprised but not amazed."

"Jim says they got rid of everything last night. Jim has

166

been off it for a week or so and he feels better already. I shouldn't be telling you all this," Kathy said. She was sober, serious. "I just . . . I wouldn't tell anyone else. You know how things buzz on this campus. Please . . . Jim would be thrown out along with Hobey."

Marion said mischievously, "Pam, why don't you make a deal with her? She lays off Willy, you keep her secret."

Pam felt herself flushing. She said, with all the dignity she could muster, "That's not funny. I have no strings on Willy."

Marion was contrite. "Hey, I didn't know it was that serious."

"What do you mean 'serious'? Goodness sake."

Now Kathy relaxed, laughing with Marion. "Pam, dear, please. You and Willy are made for each other."

"I . . . I don't think I want to talk about it."

"We know," they chorused. "Let's go make some coffee and talk about Title IX or something," said Marion.

"If you'll tote my racquets in I'll jog a bit," said Pam.

"Okay, sister. Too bad Willy's at practice."

She made a rude gesture and began jogging toward the lake. Frost had not yet applied delicate fingers to the leaves of the trees, but it would soon. She thought of how silly she had been. Why didn't she just laugh it off? Why did she have to blush? She just wasn't used to it—this new feeling— she told herself.

Now, when she jogged lakeside, she thought of him. He was so shy and yet not really afraid to speak up. It had affected her deeply and she admitted it to herself. She had always tried to be honest in herself, with herself. She had a career which would earn her more money than she would need. She was in the top ten at seventeen and she would go on from there. She owed it to her parents and to the hours she had labored. She had given up little to gain much. Boys had never interested her and she had not been interested in boys, at least not much. There was that young Italian on the tour . . . But she had been programmed to avoid any entanglements and stick to her game. She had done well with her game. She would do better, and Willy would help.

Willy—it always came back to Willy. It could throw everything out of line, throw her out of gear. It was true that she could not concentrate in the rallying with the girls because her thoughts insisted upon drifting to Willy.

She had to take a firm stand. She was conditioned to discipline. She must get her ducks in a line, get her head together, all those things that determine whether a player in any game would remain at the top or sink out of sight.

So she scolded herself.

17

THE NEXT DAY Pam worked Kathy and Marion to a frazzle, fiendishly running them from side to side, opening the center and driving between them. She had never played better.

The basketball players were not so coordinated. Tiny Petey Peale was a problem. Jones' insistence on running at all times upset a bit of the passing routines. They shot hundreds of times from the foul lines and made a discovery: Peale almost never missed. It was his best skill in practice. It remained to be seen how well he would do under pressure in a game but the coaches had high hopes.

Willy found it all a bit confusing but his adaptability, strengthened by his experience was of great help. He had learned something, he felt, by watching the Knicks—a few new tricks, a maneuver which might turn him loose inside twenty feet of the basket. He had no delusions about his ability to play with the professionals, but his close study of them matched the ambition of Coach Jones to introduce the Harper kids to at least a modicum of the machinery which was in use in the league.

On the weekend they traveled to Newark again. The opponent was Chestnut Hill, a rough and tough group, it was rumored. They went on Friday with the cheerleaders and the bus. They went onto the court feeling strong but not overconfident.

At the half the score was 40 to 40. Chestnut Hill had elected to play a wide open game. They had the muscle, as predicted, to break up the full-court press.

Jones changed the lineup in the second half. He sent Sig Ruman to forward and put Petey Peale in at guard. The Chestnut Hill fans screamed with laughter.

In three minutes Petey had been fouled four times. He had not missed a shot from the line. The opposing coach was going mad on the sidelines. The big, strong home team could not avoid fouling the swift little man. They tried bumping him and he bounced like a rubber ball. Harper lost coherence and Jones inserted Maloney again and Willy began to turn his miracles into points.

The final score was 80 for Harper, 56 for Chestnut Hill. The next night it was even worse, 82 to 50 in favor of Harper. Willy went to the coach and asked, "May I remain in town overnight?"

"You got a girl in Newark?"

"No. A friend. Brock."

"The Central High flash?"

"That's right." He hesitated, then said, "Coach, he wants to go to Harper College. I tried to get my folks to write letters. No dice. I have to tell him."

"No help, huh?"

"It's the story of my life, Coach."

Jones said, "Yeah. I guess I catch on. Look. You tell that turkey I'll write a letter for what good it'll do. And so will Holder."

170

"Hey, thanks. Thanks a heap. At least I can tell him something good."

"I wish I could have him for a year. He's right up in your class. Now don't get a swelled head. There was a couple moves you made today I wanta talk about."

"Okay, Coach. Anything you say." He was off and running, digging for the card Brock had given him.

They met in the little restaurant. Brock listened and sighed. He said, "I can get recommendations from coaches. That don't color me white. You dig?"

"Man, it's tough for me. The only way I got into Harper was through the family's donations, I'm sure of that."

"You and me, huh?" Brock grinned. "We got good grades, we're stars, but nobody much loves us."

"That's the way it goes down."

Brock said, "Okay. You like to dance?"

"Sure, why not?"

"My sister knows a honky gal from the normal school. You want to gyrate a bit? Mixed crowd. Black and tan they used to call it. Stompin' at the Savoy. Fats Waller, Duke Ellington, if they were only alive. But we got tapes and stereo. You game?"

"Love it, but I have to cut out in time to make curfew. Midnight at Harper."

"They do that number on you?"

"Stop and think, pal. We're still kids—to them. And then there's training."

"We train. But Sundays we sleep in."

"Sunday I'm playing tennis in Morristown."

"Iron Man Crowell. Okay, get you off and runnin' in my little bus so you can make it."

171

He had a good time. The people were great. He liked the girl from normal school. He liked Brock's pretty sister. The music was terrific. Everything was fine excepting that all through the evening he was thinking of Pam and how much better it would be if she were with him.

On Sunday morning Willy was telling Pam about it. "And would you believe Brock drove me all the way to school? Made it just before closing time."

She said, "What a nice young man. A normal school girl? She's going to be a teacher? Was she really pretty?"

"Oh, sure. And Brock's sister is a real beauty."

She unzipped her tennis racquet. They were on a perfectly kept court in Morristown. The weather was bright. "I'm glad you had a good time."

"It was super," he said. He drew his sweater over his head. When he could see her again she was walking rapidly to the service line of the right-hand court. He hastened to take his place across from her.

They rallied. Then Pam began serving. Her first service was a wide, swinging ace. Willy called, "Hey, great. A good court agrees with you."

She did not respond. She served a near ace which he returned weakly. She smashed to the corner. He blew the return.

She took the game without loss of a point. They changed courts. He was eyeing her with surprise. She was silent and he had no wish to break her concentration.

He served a half-speed twist. She put it away. He frowned a little now; he had not won a point. He wound up and let go his best down the line serve. She got to it. He went to the net. She anticipated and cross-courted. He barely got the strings on the ball.

He steadied down. He began to drop shot, to use the angles, to lob. He managed to win the game. She took the balls for her service, a tiny line between her brows. She delivered a flat, low service. He cut it off and applied top spin. He got the corner and the point and she was visibly annoyed.

He finally won a long, bone-wearying set at 7-6, putting away the last point of the tie-breaker with a service ace. She wiped the handle of her racquet, ready for more. She had not uttered a word during the entire session.

He sat down on a chair. "Hey, this is by far the best workout we ever had. You're on top. No more today. You could go stale."

She said icily, "I may not be pretty but I'm good at my thing."

"Wh-what?"

"I'm not great on a dance floor but my footwork is okay on a tennis court, right?"

"Hey, there, baby."

"I'm not a baby. I'm not a normal school beauty. I'm just awkward old Pamela Stern."

He looked around. Two of the courts were occupied. He gulped but managed to get an arm around her. "Pam, baby. Jealousy doesn't become you. I'd love to take you dancing, love to take you anywhere, everywhere."

She was stiff as a ramrod. "All those Hollywood girls. You were in trouble, all right. I can see that. You're just the type."

"Pam!"

Tears trickled down her face, now suddenly again childlike as he had first seen it on the bus to Morristown. "Willy."

"Hey, it was nothing—an evening with nice people."

"I know."

"Well, what then?"

"It's all so new to me. I . . . I can't seem to handle it. I never, never cared for a boy before. I never did," she wailed.

"Me too. I mean . . . like you. Never." Words came hard again.

"That's not true!"

"It's true. That girl I got in trouble with. I was drinking and smoking pot. I scarcely knew her. And they made a big thing out of nothing."

"Honest, Willy?"

"I couldn't lie to you."

"You . . . you couldn't?"

She drew a deep sobbing breath. "I think I know that. I . . . I believe that. You wouldn't."

"I couldn't."

"You . . . we're so young. But I feel it real big, Willy."

He said, "Ever since that first day on the bus it's been growing. Just . . . growing."

She gathered up her sweater and the racquets. "I want to walk to the park."

"Jog. I'm supposed to jog."

"I'll jog with you."

They trotted toward the park in the center of Morristown. Instructors were walking the prospective Seeing Eye dogs. There was a lot of traffic. Grumman appeared in the station wagon and handed them mail he had picked up at the post

174

office box. They did not open the mail. They were silent, sitting close together all the way to the school. Gus was also unnaturally quiet. They parted with a long look, smiling, a bit dubious, a bit afraid, but content.

In his room Willy opened a letter from his father. It read in part, "What's this with tennis and that eastern Jew girl? Tennis and basketball require two different sets of muscles. Don't you or the coach know that? And what's with this nigger kid? I'm not about to write a letter for a kid I don't even know, a kid from Newark yet. Is this some new thing your mother's been putting in your head? Shape up, Willy. The only good thing I hear is about your grades. That's a new one. I'm pleased, of course. Get your head together and bring Harper a championship team so you can go on to college a name, a star. . . ."

The rest of the letter didn't mean a thing to him. He ripped it up and put it in the wastebasket. He sat a long time alone, looking out the window. It was borne in upon him that the only person with whom he could really communicate on a gut level was Pam.

Hobey Barker also had a letter. He read it when he came in, sweating from his daily run. His mother wrote, "Darling Son: Are you all right? We see by the Morristown paper, always several days behind, that you are not getting much playing time. What in the world has happened? Are you ill? We are much worried but hesistated to call through the office. Please telephone us at once. . . ."

There was a check for a hundred dollars enclosed. He put the letter in his desk and went out to the telephone booth on campus and called Jackson.

"Hi there, sport," said Jackson. "How's it goin'?"

"Not good."

"You're back on the team. What's the scam on the Amboy game?"

"I haven't got any scam. Now or any other time."

"Aw, come on, sport. I need to know. Your guys are hot. What kind of point spread?"

"I couldn't care less. Just take care of my car, Jackson. That's all I ask. And don't call me or come near the school. You know I'm on probation."

"It don't go down, sport. I mean, we got a deal, see? I need that dope from you. And I got some real grass, top stuff."

"Smoke it yourself. And don't take that tone with me, either, Jackson."

"What tone, sport? I'm your pal, remember?"

"You're not my pal. I'm onto you. Keep it in mind."

There was a long pause. Then Jackson said, "You're forgettin', sport. I'm onto you, too."

The line went dead. Now Hobey was really sweating. He dragged himself to his room. Jim was looking at television where the Lakers were playing the Knicks.

Jim said, "Hey, how did it go? You sure look dragged out."

"It's not easy." He went into the shower. He had not been able to talk freely with his roommate since the argument. They were still friends on the surface but Hobey felt alone, deserted. This implied threat from Jackson deepened his anxiety. If Jackson informed on him the bottom would indeed fall out of his world.

Jim turned off the set. He too felt lonely these days. He

176

walked over to the girls' dorm and gave an imitation of a whippoorwill. Kathy came out the door and said, "You did that better back home. Out of practice?"

They walked. Jim said, "Yeah. Seems like we never talk any more. Like when we were kids."

"Hobey giving you the silent treatment these days?"

"Something like that. You still chasing Willy Crowell?"

"No. I lost that one."

"Seems like we're both losers this year."

"You got playing time against Chestnut Hill. You did good."

"Tell the coach. He's set with Sig and Cappy and Crowell and Malone and Ambs. That's his starting lineup."

"With Petey filling in sixth man."

"You said it. It'll be the same at Amboy."

"Coach is out to win 'em all now."

"It's getting to Hobey. It's really eating him out, you know?"

"Hobey's been a bad boy. At least you never quit the team."

"That's not all of it."

She said, "Brother, what are you really trying to tell me? About the beer and the pot and all? Because some of us know about that."

"Some of you? The coaches? The faculty?"

"No. Just a few of us. And . . . old Gus."

"Grumman?"

"The trash, brother. It's his job to put out the trash for the trucks. The beer cans."

"He told you?"

"I happened to see what was going down one fine morning. And I can smell grass. Remember when we experimented and I didn't like it?"

"So you told your pals."

She said, "They were wondering about you and Hobey."

"Just your close pals?"

"Marion and Pam."

"Pam? Don't you know she's Crowell's girl?"

"If I know anything," she said, "you can depend on Pam. She's a rock."

"It sure is different from last year," he mourned.

"Yes. Harper's winning basketball games."

"You don't have to rub it in."

"If it wasn't for Hobey and the junk he got you taking, everything would be like last year."

"Hey, don't blame it all on Hobey. I liked it. I was having fun."

She said, "Jim, you've stopped hitting yourself in the guts. Now stop hitting yourself over the head."

He said, "Walk you back, sis. Only I better jog in case the coach is around."

They jogged back to her dorm. He looked at her. He said, "Hey, you're my sis."

"You're my big brother."

"Hey."

"Hey."

He went back to his room. Hobey was studying. Jim went into the shower, feeling better than he had in several weeks.

18

THE TEAM PLAYED Amboy School. In the first game Maloney turned an ankle. Jones said, "North, go in."

Willy took an inbound from Cappy and went through the Amboys and scored. Amboy brought it out and Willy blocked a pass. North took it and gave to Cappy. Willy was double-teamed. North sprinted under the basket, jumped, took the toss from Cappy and scored.

Amboy never closed the gap. Everyone on the Harper team excepting Hobey Barker got into the game.

The next day it was the same. Willy found a weakness in the defense of the other team and roared up and down the court. The lead became twenty points.

Jones said, "All right. Rohm, Alexander, Field, North . . . Barker."

Hobey sat for a moment, unbelieving. There were five minutes to play. For a moment it seemed he would not doff his warm-up garments. Then he was on the court.

Amboy, resentful at facing substitutes, began to play over their heads. Two of Hobey's shots were blocked in desperation moves. Nevertheless, he ran and rebounded and covered his man on defense and Harper won by sixteen points.

Afterwards, in the dressing room, Jones was calm but pleased. "I think we got a team here. You played like a

179

team. You acted like a team. North and Barker, you're in better shape, for some reason or other. Could it be you're runnin' a lot?"

They nodded assent. They were subdued but not cowed.

Cappy said, "I figure it's Battin or us. They lost only one game in the conference—to us. And they gave Central a fit."

"They didn't beat Central. Brock was too much," said Sig. "That Brock is the best player we've faced all season."

Coach Jones asked, "Would your parents say that in a letter to Harper College? Anybody?"

"He wants to go to Harper?"

"He's got the grades. He could make the team a winner," said Jones.

Willy said, "And he's a really nice guy. His family is nice. There's no reason he shouldn't go to Harper."

No one spoke. They all dressed and went their respectful ways. Willy remained behind with Jones.

He said, "Coach, that was a swell try."

"It's been on my mind. Tell you what else." He looked around to make sure they were alone. "I wouldn't mind goin' over there myself."

"No kidding. I thought you wanted back to the pros."

The big man was a bit embarrassed. "Never worked with kids before. College—they're still kids. And . . . well, you guys are goin' up there. Most of you."

Willy put a hand on the coach's shoulder. "That's the nicest thing a coach ever said to me. Thanks."

"Things start out rough. You make 'em what you can. If you can give somethin' and feel somethin' coming back . . . It's a great feelin', Crowell."

180

"I'm beginning to learn that myself. And I've got you to thank for a lot of it," Willy told him.

They walked from the gym together, instinctively broke into a trot, laughed, and went their separate ways.

Mrs. Cross was waving a letter. Botley surveyed her with jaundiced eye.

"This is from the parents of Hobart Barker. It demands an answer."

"Very well. Since you received it, you may answer it."

"They wish to know why he is not playing in the games."

"He played today."

"For a few paltry minutes."

"Did they ask why he is confined to campus and on probation with the coach?"

"They . . ." She stopped. Then she said, "I—uh—suppose they have not been informed."

"Yes. I see. Then you should inform them."

"Really! I am not the dean."

"But you would like to be Dean of Women. You are efficient, Mrs. Cross. But lately you seem to be crusading, wouldn't you say?"

"I have been enduring pressure from such as Pamela Stern, who wants more and more privileges for the girls. I have been harassed by a so-called committee dealing with Title IX. Crusading? I have been essaying to maintain sanity and a semblance of order."

"Mrs. Cross, I have put myself in a precarious position by hiring a competent basketball coach. Thus far the venture is successful. Please believe me, all will be in the balance when and if Mrs. Harper returns from Europe. Until then it is best to maintain the status quo. As to Barker and his parents, since you are so close to the boy I leave it up to you. Answer the letter."

"Even if I think Hobart is being discriminated against?"

He smiled slightly. "That is again a matter of judgment."

"My judgment." She wrinkled the tip of her nose. "Very well. Harper School needs funds. I will act accordingly."

"Again—your decision."

She flounced out of the office. He returned to his favorite view of the campus. He was not at all certain that he was acting in the best interest of himself. He was almost sure that he was doing his best for the school.

The basketball team played Miller Prep. They won both games. North and Barker played as substitutes. Each was gaining strength; neither showed signs of exhaustion. Petey Peale was enormously useful in spots. Ambs grew stronger under the boards. And Willy scored and scored.

They played Madison High and ran into early trouble when a great outside shooter named Gorman made some miraculous shots in the first period. Cappy and Sig went to work on him, Peale ran circles around the Madison defense, and Willy found openings from which he could shoot. Again, Harper won both games.

Battin School was keeping pace. The sports pages were full of praise for the reigning champions. Life went on at Harper as the season changed and autumn finally came with its outrageously beautiful shades of brown and red and yellow. Barker and North continued to run. More and more

Coach Jones called upon them in spots. The team had become an eleven-player unit.

Pam and Willy now were welcome at a new indoor tennis complex in Morristown. Tennis enthusiasts gathered on Sunday to watch and sometimes participate in mixed doubles with Marion and a local club champion or near champion. Pam's game steadily improved. Indeed, Willy's skills were enhanced through these hard competitive workouts.

Borden Military came to Harper and left defeated. Harper went to Gladstone in the Jersey hills and was victorious. All teams began the second round of play in November and snow fell and Willy rose early in the mornings to enjoy the beauty of the landscape, the trees bending under the burden of icicles, the drifts resembling the sand dunes of the West Coast. He adjusted well to the cold weather. He felt strong and confident in his new and different life. He heard little from his parents, which was nothing new to him.

Then the holiday season approached, with excitement growing as the student body en masse prepared to go home for Christmas. That was when Willy did receive word from home. There were two carefully wrapped packages, one large, one small, with little notes attached to the outsides. The one from his mother said, "Notice is up, show closing. Will, unfortunately, be in the Bahamas for Xmas. Love and kisses. Call me . . . Mother."

From his father it was, "Taking off for a film in Durango. Keep up the good work on the courts."

He showed them to Pam, not opening the gifts. "I'm not going home either," she told him. "We'll have the place to ourselves."

"It'll be the best Christmas I've had in many a year," he told her. "I can scarcely remember my last tree."

"We'll put one up in the rec hall," she promised. "Just for us chickens." She did not tell him that she was framing excuses to her family in order to remain at Harper. "I made some enquiries. Botley, Coach Jones, and Grumman will be here. Maybe a couple of others."

"Most everyone has a family."

She said quickly, "Now, Willy."

"It's all right. I wouldn't know anything different."

"So . . . I'll ask permission to put up a tree. And Gus will help. And we can pick up gag presents in Morristown." She was off and running, full of plans.

He already had her gift, selected from a catalogue and purchased through the mail. He went to his room feeling somewhat exhilarated. She had the ability to influence his moods.

Sig said, "Hey, I'm sorry you're going to be stuck here."

"Forget it. We've got ideas."

"I know. But, shoot, Christmas is family. My kid brother and two sisters, they'd be sick if I wasn't there. To say nothing of ma and pa."

"Sure, I know. Figure it this way. What you never had you don't miss." He had heard the expression before. It was the first time he believed it.

They had two games with Amboy just prior to the vacation. They romped home by large margins. Coach Jones was more than pleased. Botley congratulated him with enthusiasm.

184

Hobey Barker wrote a check for car storage in Jackson's office. When he handed it over the garage owner said, "So you're off probation and all. What about the rest of the games? What about Battin?"

"I told you I'm through with betting."

"You told me. But I'm not. I been doin' pretty good without your help. But I'm fixin' to get down heavy on Battin. I got to make sure."

"No way."

"Oh, yes, there's a way. You're gettin' more playin' time, you and North."

"So what?"

"Your team's improved. But so has Battin. It's gonna be a toss-up. I want the edge."

"You have to be kidding."

"I never joke about money. What I want—since you're gonna lose anyway—I want the points shaved."

Hobey came to his feet, his neck swelling. "Now just a damn minute here, Jackson."

Jackson grinned at him. "Lay a hand on me and you're dead. Don't you know that?"

"I'll wipe you out if you . . ."

Jackson said, "When you get in that game you don't score. Not you, not North. Jones uses you two in spots and, with Crowell a threat, you been countin' pretty good. Forget it. You miss."

"You're out of your stupid head."

"Look at it this way. I blow the whistle. I go to Botley. I tell him you were bettin' against your own team. I got proof,

185

don't you worry." He uncovered a small machine. "A recorder, see? Every time you called in I got it on tape. You see what I mean, Barker?"

"Why you . . ." He made a grab for the recorder. Jackson produced a tire iron.

"Touch it and I'll break your arm."

Hobey felt the blood draining from his face. "If you tell on me you're telling on yourself."

"I got a 'For Sale' sign goin' up in the morning," Jackson said. "This burg is gettin' too small for me. I got connections. Fact is, if you don't do like I say these certain people will take care of you sooner or later."

Cold fear stabbed at Hobey. "Connections?"

"You think I'm workin' alone? I'm too smart for that."

Hobey said, "You dirty . . ."

"Call me names, it gets you nothin'. It's the money I'm after. Now just run along and think it over. Think what your people will say. Think about gettin' thrown outa school on your butt. Think about playin' any more basketball anywhere in the world. Read up on the old basketball fixes. And get smart, Barker, get smart."

Hobey went out into the wintry sunlight. A cold wind thrust against him. He walked to the bus station which would take him to the airport in Newark. He scarcely noticed the suitcase he was carrying. He was numb. And he was terribly afraid.

The tree was fat and thick with pine needles. Pam and Willy and Gus had found ornaments in a Morristown store.

186

They gathered around and drank soft beverages and toasted one another. Botley was overcome.

"No one ever thought of it before. They run off to the bosoms of their families and forget us."

"These two, Pam and Willy, they did it all," said Gus.

Coach Jones looked at the red and white winter sweater which was his gift, and knotted a big fist. "Willy Crowell, you came here and it went hard for you. They dragged at you so that I didn't think you could handle it. You came through."

Willy said, "Thanks, Coach. Maybe I'm learning early that time takes care of a lot."

"They don't even bother him for autographs any more," Pam said. "And you, Coach, you con't criticize his tennis workouts."

"And you two get grades," Botley said. "Good grades. You will make the college boards with ease. Harper, I hope?"

"I'll be going there," said Willy. "And I want Brock of Central High there."

Botley cleared his throat. "I don't know how much good it will do. But I've decided to put in a word."

"I'm sure that you and Coach will have some influence," Pam said.

"And you? Are you going on to Harper College?"

"I was in doubt." She paused, frowning. "It's both a pleasure and a family duty to play on the tour. Attending classes full time would destroy me. I'll promise this: When I can attend, it will be at Harper."

"That's all we can ask," said Botley. "I'm afraid we've done little or nothing for you here. You've brought international attention to the school. We haven't been able to return in kind."

She said, "Harper's given me happiness. It's changed me, brought me out of myself."

"Thanks to Willy," said Grumman gruffly. "I know a thing or two about folks. You two make a great pair."

They were both flushing. They did not flinch, however. They stood together at the tree. He had given her a gold necklace with her intitials on one side of the locket and his on the other. She had presented him with a thin gold brace-let.

She said, "We haven't opened Willy's presents from his folks."

"Golly, I plumb forgot." He opened the large one from his mother. It contained ski clothing purchased at Saks Fifth Avenue. "I'm supposed to pack in the Sierras next summer," he explained. "Mother thinks there's skiing all year around wherever there are mountains."

He opened the smaller package. It contained a wristwatch which gave digital time, the day of the week, the month, everything which could be crowded upon an oversize crystal. He said, "That's the third one he's given me. His mind runs in a channel." He peered at it. "A stopwatch? Coach, do me a favor? Take this off my hands."

"Oh, no, I couldn't do that."

Willy turned it over. "You see? No initials, no inscription. Please, Coach, I'm serious."

There was a small silence. Then Jones held out his burly

wrist and Willy fastened the heavy leather strap. "You see? On you it looks good."

When the party was over Pam walked back to the dorm at his side. "You don't hate your father, do you?"

"No. I don't hate him. I just don't like him very much."

"He meant well. It's a beautiful watch."

"Not beautiful. Expensive."

"Still . . ."

"Pam, you have to understand. Truly, I'd much rather the coach wore it. It'll be useful to him. He's a nice guy. And . . . he'll remember Willy when he looks at it. That's a fine Christmas present to me."

"Yes. I see."

"I wouldn't have thought like that when I came here. I guess I did hate father. Mother, she's foolish and rattle-brained and wrong about a lot of things. But I always knew I loved her. Father is . . . I often thought . . . hoped . . . he wasn't my real father. Oh, he is all right. But he's not a real man. He's an actor."

"And your mother's an actress."

"I know. I haven't got all the answers. I just know I love my mother and I don't love my father."

"Maybe some day."

"I'd have said no to that before I met you."

"Willy, it's getting pretty heavy between us." She touched the gold necklace with one finger. "We must be careful."

"I know. When I think of you going on the tour and me hiking in the mountains . . . It hurts."

189

"Growing up. We're growing up. They tell us that it always hurts."

At the entry to her dorm he pulled her close. They stood that way for a long time. It began to snow—light, star-shaped flakes. They lifted their faces and tasted it on the tips of their tongues. Then they kissed, long and gently and warmly.

She said, "I hope we grow up right."

"Let's work on it, Pam dear. Let's work hard at it."

She went indoors. He walked through the snow, trying hard to put it all in place. He had been through so many low valleys that he was slightly afraid of the heights.

19

WILLY SHIVERED as the sleet drove against the window of the bus. The driver could scarcely see through the windshield. They were bound, oddly, for Central High School in Newark. The conference had decided that the play-off game between Harper and Battin for the championship should be held on neutral ground. Central had been chosen because of its large capacity for the fans, and because it had seemed most economical to hold the big event in Newark.

Sig said, "Great idea this was. We'll freeze in that old barn, you know that?"

Willy was wearing the ski clothing his mother had given him. He was still chilled, his nose ran; he had never been in exactly this kind of weather. "We won't be overheated. It sure will feel good to run."

"We been running so long I dream about it. Like I'm trying to get up this hill and my legs are giving out."

"We're almost to the top of the hill. One more game."

"Did you notice Hobey hasn't been playing his game this week? I mean, like there's something on his mind?"

"Coach noticed it. He's been working on him."

"North hasn't been all that sharp either."

"Maybe they got worn down with the running. Discipline is not their strong point."

"We need them in spots. They were getting to be real good there toward the end of the season."

"Real good," Willy agreed. "Gave Maloney and you and Petey plenty of rest."

"It worked. Coach was right."

"All the way."

"Run, run run. Hey, you're not a bit uptight, are you?"

"Nope."

"I'm scared. After last year . . . then this great season . . . I'm scared it won't last."

"We play the game, pal."

"Why do I feel so . . . responsible?"

"Part of the game. Maybe that's why it's good to play."

Sig was quiet for awhile, moving restlessly in the seat, his brow wrinkled. "If any one of us don't come through," he said finally, "it's going to be Pitsville."

"Uh-huh." Willy was thinking of Pam in the station wagon, taking her first trip to a game away from Harper. She would also have the nervous jitters. She was cool on the tennis court but she wanted the team to win as much as she had ever wanted a trophy for herself. She was not only a great girl, she was a great person. He remembered her unstated sympathy after the encounter with his mother—more sympathy than he needed or deserved, he thought.

He thought about Steve Brock. At least Steve had a loyal family. Whether or not he made it to Harper College, he would be all right. But it would be so much better to have him as a teammate and friend, someone with whom he could communicate on a day-to-day basis.

Not that he could not communicate with Sig and Cappy,

192

mainly Sig. The notoriety had interfered with his attempt to be outgoing, to mix on equal terms with the others. But the furor had died down. Young people did not cling to scandal—not to much else, he thought. They were too busy living.

He had learned a lot at Harper. He could not evaluate how much he had learned but he knew it was worthwhile. It had softened the edge of his disappointment at the hands of his parents when they refused to endorse Brock, when his mother had run to Brevoort that night at the theatre.

He could not be uptight about the game with Battin. He was, he supposed, more mature than Sig and the others. It did not sadden him to realize this was true. He looked down the aisle at Barker and North and felt sympathy for them. They had hurt themselves more than they had harmed the team. They could not be happy with this knowledge.

They were sitting side by side without words. Hobey was frightened. The swaggering confidence that had carried him so long was evaporated. Jim was more composed. He knew the situation was desperate. He knew that if Hobey was exposed as a bettor against the team that he would be involved. But Jim had given his best for most of the season; he had that upon which to fall back. He had found a certain courage deep inside him which he had not known he possessed.

The bus came to High Street and parked at Central High. The station wagon had preceded it and the faculty, Gus, Mrs. Cross, Botley, Pam, and some others formed a lane as the cheerleaders followed Kathy to leap and yell.

It was freezing cold when Willy came down the three

steps of the bus. Suddenly there was a change in the cheering as a dozen boys and girls, led by Steve Brock, thrust forward, waving Harper pennants. The Harper team stopped dead. Then they raised their fists and yelled back, "Hey, Central!"

Steve came as close as possible and called, "After the game, California. Win, lose, or draw?"

"Right on," said Willy. At last he felt a thrill, a tingling in his bloodstream, an anticipation of the contest to come. The sportsmanship, the friendliness of the one team which had twice won victories over Harper, made everything come alive and clear. He trotted into the school and down to the dressing room, light-headed, wings on his feet.

Outside the school on the cold, icy sidewalk Pam danced a little jig and asked, "Please, Gus, can't we go indoors?"

Gus Grumman said, "Now just hold on, young lady. You'll be glad you waited."

"I don't want to wait."

"Willy will be in the dressing room for an hour," he told her, winking and grinning.

"I'm freezing."

"You'll warm up. . . . Ah, there!"

A taxicab pulled up to the curb. Gus ran to open the door. A lady in a full-length mink coat stepped out and took his hand. She wore a smart, toque chapeau over close-cut white hair. Her face was bright with the chill of the evening and her eyes were sharp but kindly. She saw Pam and came striding, arms outstretched.

"Mrs. Harper!" Pam flew into the embrace.

"Pamela, darling."

194

"You're here. You're actually home."

"Thank Gus. He sent me a cable some time ago."

"A cable?"

"Things was goin' pretty bad. Don't like things right now," Gus said. "There's problems."

"But the team did well," said Mrs. Harper, pride in her voice. "Mr. Botley made the right decision when he employed Mr. Jones."

"Oh, yes," said Pam. "And when they brought in Willy Crowell. Oh, yes, indeed."

"Shall we go in?"

Gus said, "Three seats right behind the scorer's table. They better be ready for us."

They were ready. Botley came to his feet, staring. Mrs. Cross swallowed hard, tried to smile. The cheerleaders were on the floor. Kathy took one look, gulped, gathered them, danced out, and lifted her arms high.

"Mrs. Harper! Our Mrs. Harper! Let's hear it!"

The school cheer rang out. The Battin fans applauded. One by one the crowd struggled to arise and salute the lady well-known and well-liked throughout the state.

Mrs. Harper lifted both hands, mitting them like a champion prizefighter, flashing her smile. When the hubbub had ceased she sat down and turned to Gus.

"You'd better tell me. In my ear, Gus. Your best whisper."

The whisper was a low growl. Pam could hear part of it. "Barker and North . . . beer . . . marijuana . . . pickin' on Crowell . . . Wait'll you see Crowell, Miz Harper . . . Fella name of Jackson in town . . . You know I ain't no

195

snoopin' squealer but it needed some lookin' into . . . That Cross woman . . . Crowell and Pam . . ."

She found herself blushing again and closed her ears firmly against any further eavesdropping. Kathy and the girls were doing their formations, gyrations, arm-waving gymnastics, and the little band was playing the school song in disco rhythm. She saw Brock and the entire Central High squad sitting not far from her own place. They were following the Harper cheers from memory. The officials in their zebra-striped shirts were coming onto the floor. Excitement built and she clenched her hands.

Mrs. Harper said, "Thank you, Gus. You acted precisely as I should have wanted."

"There may be some shinanigans comin' up. I seen that Jackson and a couple others come in here tonight."

"Not to worry, Gus. We'll see what happens and act accordingly."

The teams were coming onto the court. They were introduced, first the Battin boys, then Harper's squad. Mrs. Harper leaned forward, intent, her sharp eyes scanning the boys in red and white. When Willy came on and the crowd began yelling "California," she sat back.

"So that's your young man," she said.

Pamela said, "Oh, no. Not so."

"Don't believe her," said Gus. "Miz Cross is dyin' to tell you how they were canoodlin' by the lake."

"Gus!"

He chuckled. "They're a mighty handsome pair, ain't they, Miz Harper?"

"You're always right, Gus." She winked, made a droll face

196

at Pamela. "Finally a boy appreciates you, dear. I always wondered how they could be so blind."

"She never encouraged them none," said Gus.

Pam said, "Gus, you know too much."

The teams were ready on the court. The trio behind the scorer's table became silent, tense, watching. Coach Jones stood tall, looking up at them. He saluted, sat down. Willy also looked, raised an arm to Pam. She gave him the victory sign.

Willy found himself confronted not by Hartner but by Fortney. Battin had altered formation, putting star against star. It made for a different strategy.

The horn started, the ball went up. Diamond got the tap for Battin. It came back to Fortney. Willy moved in. Fortney protected the ball. Harper went into the full-court press. Fortney attempted to go past Willy. Sig darted in to help and Fortney slipped a foot out of bounds.

Cappy came up to inbound. His fake to Willy and Fortney was right on the spot. Cappy gave to Sig, who went to Maloney, who went to Ambs on the high post. Willy flew down the lane. Fortney covered him with great skill, playing him close. Ambs found Sig, Cappy rolled away from Grange and jumped. His shot went cleanly through the hoop and Harper had drawn first blood. Willy was down the court as Battin tried the fast break.

Fortney made a new move, clever and quick. He got loose for a split second. He scored.

Cappy gave to Willy again. Battin fell back into a zone. Willy held up two fingers, a signal for a crisscross. Sig went to the left. Maloney went to the right. Ambs got in deep beneath the basket. Fortney came out to tackle Willy, who evaded with the nimble move of a bullfighter. Cappy bulled his way close. Willy gave him a low pass. They double-teamed Cappy but Fortney could not stay with Willy. Cappy slid the ball so low it almost rolled into Willy's grasp. Straightening, Willy went over Fortney and put the ball into the net.

Mrs. Harper said, "I see what you people mean. The boy from California is something else again, is he not?"

Pam was screaming, "Go, Willy, go!"

Gus said, "Like I told you, ma'am."

The Central High gang was whooping it up. Brock was waving his arms and leading them in a chant. "California, California, California!"

Pam leaned toward Mrs. Harper. "That boy, the handsome one leading the Central High crowd? He wants to go to Harper College. He and Willy are friends."

"Those are the boys that beat us?"

"Specially Brock," Pam said. "He's an A student, too."

Mrs. Harper smiled broadly, patting Pam's hand. "My goodness, things are really picking up in old New Jersey."

On the court the battle went on. The two teams were so evenly matched that the spectators were on the edge of their seats every moment of the action. The Battin bench came on. Jones put in North and Petey Peale. Petey was overmatched but he sneaked in for a score, then was fouled. A moment later North fouled Fortney, who was overpowering him.

Jones replaced Petey with Barker. Willy came down with

198

the ball again, giving the signal for a play against the zone. Barker missed the signal, then recovered and got loose. Willy sent him a high hard pass. Barker leaped and shot. The ball rolled around the iron—and failed to go in.

Diamond wrestled the rebound. Battin went flying down and Hartner scored as Willy covered Fortney. The Battin stands went crazy as they led for the first time in the game.

They continued to hold the two-point advantage until the half. It had been a high-scoring, all-out contest, 45 to 43. The teams retired to the locker rooms, the girls and the band took the floor.

Mrs. Harper said to Gus, "Hobey was trying to make that basket. You know that."

"Yeah. He was tryin'," said Gus. "Too close for it to be intended to miss."

"Where is the man Jackson?"

"Up high. Right on the lane where the boys come out to play."

"Why, I know the man. He worked on my car last year."

"Yes, ma'am. I took the car in for you."

"Gus, you are a detective in your heart."

"A Marine, ma'am."

She laughed. They chatted through the intermission. The tension in the gym was enormous. They tried to ignore it but Pam felt it, worried about the team, about Willy, about what might be about to happen. She had heard enough to know that something evil was afoot. She looked at Jackson, at the two toughs who sat on either side of him. Then she looked at Gus, who seemed calm enough under the circumstances.

Mrs. Harper said, "It's going to go down to the wire. Those Battin boys, I remember them. Fortney destroyed us last year."

"He's not destroying Willy," Pam blurted. Then she was blushing again, feeling foolish, as though she were a kid back in grade school talking out of turn. But Mrs. Harper made a face at her and she had to giggle. It did not prevent her hands from perspiring. The familiar click-click of a newsman's camera restored her composure. Gus had vanished. A sportswriter had taken his place.

Mrs. Harper said genially, "No, Harper School is not going in for a huge sports program. We are working for enough funds to honor Title IX. We intend to improve our scholastic program." She gestured. "Basketball is obviously helping to bring our small school to public attention."

"No football team?" asked the reporter.

"In the future, perhaps. We have high hopes."

"This Crowell, from California, was he recruited?"

"Absolutely not. His . . . er . . . his father attended Harper College before Harper School was founded."

"Rex Ball, that is. The movie star."

"Correct."

"Any further comment on Mr. Ball, that is, Crowell?"

"None." Her chin firmed; she stared at the young man. "I think you had better direct your questions to our tennis champion now."

Pam answered the queries mechanically. She had learned on the tour just how to handle newspapermen. She smiled and was noncommittal in the most polite manner. Gus re-

200

turned, scowling. The teams were coming on. The men of the press departed.

Mrs. Harper said, "You are a truly grown-up young lady, Pam. Thank you for taking the ball and carrying it."

"Thank you for being here. We need you."

Hobey Barker came to the bench and listened to the coach's last instructions. More defense was the cry. He could not get his mind in order. His long happy life was endangered. He had never before been forced to face such danger. He had always been confident, oblivious of rules, carefree in the glow of the admiration and devotion of his family. Now he could not lean upon them; he was on his own. He could see Jackson and the other two men staring down at him. He shuddered.

The team circled for the traditional garland of hand-touching. Hobey found himself next to Willy. He felt the warm grasp of the big paw, looked at Willy's calm countenance. Impulsively, Hobey said, "Get 'em, California."

Willy nodded and went onto the court. Fortney grinned at him and asked, "Any way to stop you, Crowell?"

"Kill me." Willy returned the grin.

The ball went ceilingward, Ambs outjumped Diamond, Willy had the ball. Fortney was atop him. Willy gave him the head fake and Fortney did not go for it. Willy dribbled to the sideline, dragged a leg. Fortney went a half-step leftward. Willy was gone past the black line, down the lane.

Cappy was covered. Maloney was open. Willy passed to Maloney, who was immediately forced outside by man-to-man. Battin had deserted the zone. Willy moved as always, ducking here, striding there, backstepping. Maloney found Sig, who penetrated to the foul line, was covered by Hartner, looked for Willy, found him guarded but flung the ball high.

Willy went up into the air and shot before gravity brought him down. The ball sailed through and it was 45 to 45 and Brock's voice could be heard above all others, "California!"

It was now, as Coach Jones had said, a matter of defense. The Battin team, experienced, well-coached, brought the ball into their court with disciplined dispatch. Fortney writhed and twisted, trying to lose Willy. It was in vain. The ball went around the figure eight. Ambs stood staunch, moving in and out of the lane like an automaton.

Then Hartner, coming from nowhere, put a pick on Willy. Fortney took a pass from Diamond and shot a twenty-foot brilliant basket and Battin led by two.

Willy said to Fortney. "You don't have to kill me. You're bad, man, bad."

They were going back and forth again. Defense was not working. Each team scored in turn. Jones called for time.

At the bench he said, "North, Peale, get in there. Defense is not working. Get points."

It did not seem quite right to Willy but he went to work. Fortney was a great player. It was like shaking off iron shackles to get loose from him. Once he slipped and Willy got loose for a pass and there was Fortney backing at the ball.

Willy offered it to him like a Harlem Globetrotter, yanked it back. He pivoted from twenty-five feet out. No one was open. Willy set himself and gambled the shot.

202

He scored. Harper was even at 47 points. Peale went out. North came in. Battin scored.

Willy dribbled it down, saw North loose, gave him a straight, chest-high pass. North flipped it into the hoop.

Battin went into the fast break and Fortney was there again, counting two points as Willy feared to foul him. The crowd was screaming, voices becoming hoarse at the nip-and-tuck battle.

Pam said, "I don't know how much more of this I can take."

"Nor I." Mrs. Harper's cheeks were flushed, her hands balled into fists.

Gus was silent, glancing from time to time at the runway to the dressing rooms, fidgeting. The score mounted. It was 70 points for each. Time was running out. Now the defense tightened as both teams looked for that last shot, the one that would win the game. There was a scramble under the Battin basket and Maloney went down. When he got up he was limping.

Jones sent in Hobey Barker. Sig was playing the other forward, Cappy in back court with Willy, Ambs at center. The game roared on as the tensions rose. Each team was watching the clock now, each maneuvering for that one basket which would determine the result, avoiding the foul that would undoubtedly tip the balance. Fortney was playing with utter brilliance. Willy could find no way to scoring position.

Barker had not played enough time against Battin for them to know him, to appreciate his skill, Willy thought. So thinking, he ran a circle, drawing Fortney out. Almost at midcourt he spun. One eye told him time was running out and they would be in overtime if Harper did not make this last shot.

He found Barker when Grange came out to double-team him with Fortney. He sent the ball flying past Grange. Barker caught it. He was unguarded for that one precious second. The basket was open, he had time. He took his time. He loosed his shot.

The ball hit the rim. It was palpably not going in. Willy was already on the run for the board. He went past Diamond and leaped.

The ball came to his hands. He plopped it into the basket.

The horn sounded. The game was over. Harper had won the conference championship for the first time in history. Steve Brock led the fans from the stands as they overflowed the floor, grabbing for Willy.

Willy was staring at Barker. He had never seen a man so forlorn, so alone, so self-defeated. He reached out a long arm. He caught Barker's shoulder. "Hey, man. You were going for both those you missed."

Barker shook his head. He had missed the shots. But now he was burdened beyond his capacity. Had he unconsciously missed? He had made those same shots a thousand times. Had he wanted to miss? He had tried; Willy was right. A keen basketball player could not be fooled. Yes, he had tried. But . . . he would never know what had caused his near misses.

He looked for Jackson as the crowds cheered and milled. There were two big men showing badges. Jackson and his companion's looked scared. The two big men produced shining handcuffs.

Hobey ran for the locker room. There was no escaping. Jackson would talk, no question about it. Jim North turned a stricken face to him. The two friends ran and changed clothes without showering. They were gone when the team burst in, full of the joy of winning.

Back at Harper a group gathered in Botley's office. It was the morning after the game. Mrs. Harper sat behind the desk. Coach Jones, Coach Holder, Mrs. Cross, Kathy, Pam, and Willy were present.

Mrs. Harper said, "No one is sorrier than I about Hobey and Jim. They chose to go home to their families. Yet I wonder if that is not where their problems began."

Kathy's eyes were red from weeping. "Jim . . . Jim and I are both spoiled, I guess. But Jim is a good boy, Mrs. Harper."

"Jackson said that they bet against the team." Mrs. Harper shook her head. "I know Jim tried to straighten out. It was too late, Kathy. They will not be back."

"I know . . . I know." She bit her lip and left the room.

Pam said, "It shouldn't be held against her. She's a fine girl."

"No, of course not. We are all here for that purpose. To keep this quiet for the sake of those two boys. Gus has told me of other matters, of which I will not speak even to those who are here." She stared at Mrs. Cross. "I believe you have something to say?"

The end of the long nose twitched. Mrs. Cross said, "I'm resigning at the end of the term."

"Sooner, I think. You will have full pay but I suggest you leave us as soon as possible."

Now Mrs. Cross fled, sniffing, in tears.

Mrs. Harper said, "That takes care of all the unpleasant matters I think. Jackson is in jail for making book and corrupting minors. I will try to make things easier for Hobey and Jim by talking with their parents. Now, for the good that has come to us all."

Coach Jones said, "You don't know me, Mrs. Harper. But I want to tell you how great these boys have been—my boys. And how Crowell held up and then put it all together. I don't want all the credit."

She nodded. "I'm happy to welcome you to Harper. I'm sure we won't be able to hold you very long. The colleges or the professionals will be after you. Mr. Botley, you made a wise move. I've already had calls from the alumni offering contributions to maintain the excellence of our sports programs. That includes you, Pamela."

"I'll be going on the tour before commencement," said Pam. "But I'll make up grades. I mean to enter the college."

Mrs. Harper smiled broadly. "You're a very quiet young man, Willy Crowell. Are you aiming for Harper College?"

"Yes, ma'am. With Steve Brock. And thank you for acting so quick. He's taking the college boards this week."

"Harper College is also broadening its athletic program." She cocked an eye at Pam. "Title IX will be implemented there as well as here. Are we all happy now?"

They accepted dismissal. She watched as Pam and Willy left together, sighed, shook her head. Then she was deep into the reports Botley had made ready for her.

On the campus it was still below 30 degrees. Pam and Willy, bundled to their ears, walked through slush to the lake. The bench was wet. Willy dried it with a scarf. They sat down.

She said, "You found a lot at Harper."

"A family. I never had a family."

"And thought you didn't need one."

"I had to think that way. Now I know. We need people."

She said, "We've got until the spring tennis tours begin."

"In July I'll be backpacking in the Sierras," he told her. "Later . . . who knows?"

"There'll be tournaments in California."

"Yes."

He put his arm around her. She nestled close. A winter sparrow came and chirped at them. There was a lifetime ahead and now they both had confidence in it and in themselves.